hogtown
bonbons

greg
kramer

The stories originally published in *Xtra!*,
Toronto's gay and lesbian bi-weekly

The Riverbank Press

Text illustrations © Greg Kramer

Cover and text design: John Terauds

THE CANADA COUNCIL | LE CONSEIL DES ARTS
FOR THE ARTS | DU CANADA
SINCE 1957 | DEPUIS 1957

We acknowledge the support of the Canada Council for the Arts for our publishing program.

Canadian Cataloguing in Publication Data

Kramer, Greg, 1961-
   Hogtown bonbons

ISBN 1-896332-11-0

I. Title.

PS8571.R356H63 1999   C813'.54   C99-931373-8
PR9199.3.K72H63 1999

The Riverbank Press
P.O. Box 456, 31 Adelaide St. E., Toronto, Ontario, Canada M5C 2J5

Printed and bound in Canada by Métrolitho

To James St Bass, Richard Cliff, Kenzia, LN,
Clark Render, David Walberg, everyone at *Xtra!*,
and the unnameable yet insistent God of Deadlines . . .

Introduction

In the spring of 1998, *Xtra!* publisher David Walberg approached
Greg Kramer to write a serial novel for the Toronto gay and
lesbian newspaper. Greg was the obvious choice for the job; the
peripatetic performer had already published two well-received
novels, *the pursemonger of fugu*, a screwball murder mystery, and
the unexpectedly dark and haunting *Couchwarmer*. Both were set
in the demimonde of Toronto's downtown art and club scene, with
characters named after city intersections: Phoebe Spadina,
Adelaide Simcoe, Alexander Church. So who better to chronicle
queer urban life for the notorious publication?

I eagerly signed on as Greg's editor and for a year had the
pleasure of overseeing the creation of *Hogtown Bonbons*, six loosely
connected vignettes that careened, with equal measures of
humour and pathos, from a Pride Day murder and a Halloween
near overdose to a New Year's party in a drunk tank and a lesbian
summer fling at a bathhouse.

If life is a box of chocolates, the confections Greg delivered
to me every two weeks were a Laura Secord mix of ecstasy-laced
coconut crunches, tooth-marked raspberry creams and liqueur-
filled mocha swirls. Greg's characters – a vengeful nurse, an
amnesiac dyke, a dozen Elvis impersonators and a cult of

tearoom-cruising Christians, among others – were usually drug-addled, often promiscuous, occasionally nasty and always wonderfully human.

With the series wrapping up as I write this, I miss these characters already. How lucky for us fans to find the entire *Hogtown Bonbons* collection in this book. Bite in and enjoy.

Rachel Giese

May 1999

the bonbons

the speckled boa

(A Johnny-on-the-spot Mystery)

The feather boa in question is two metres, three inches long and plump as an industrial vacuum hose. It's old – very old – and resides coiled up in a hatbox on the top shelf of the upstairs closet.

A more evil mantle would be hard to find. It's steeped in the blessed perfumes of a thousand drag queens. It has survived the wars.

Its core is rubber – similar to that tough rubber they use for hot-water bottles. Its body is primarily black ostrich, spattered with a handful of peacock feathers. Those turquoise-and-gold flashes amid the black plume look like the eyes of predators glinting in the forest!

▼

The Annual Church Street County Fair is in full swing and, guess what? It's hot. God may favour homosexuals with glorious clear skies, but the Devil surely has shares in sunscreen and bottled water. The crowd, somewhere around the million mark, smells of roasting flesh and coconut oil. Perhaps this year it's all just a wee bit too popular for comfort.

The parade has nearly finished. Soon the poor people tending the craft-and-worthy-cause tables at the bottom of the street won't know what hit them. Already the top of the street is experiencing a sudden flood of steamy, sweaty humans to shame the Mississippi. Huckleberry of Finland types ride on shoulders and clamber up lampposts. An elderly lady, caught in the thick of it, looks as if she's disco dancing with her arms above her wisteria-dyed head – but she isn't.

It happened that quickly. One minute the street was scattered with a handful of casual wanderers, the next there was this: one million homosexual men, lesbians, and their sympathizers trying to force themselves down a street too narrow to accommodate them all.

Three blocks further south it's like the calm and peaceful Alpine village before an avalanche hits.

"Of course it's got no fucking meat products in it."

Charlie slams a turkey sausage into a bun, then hands it over, smiling at the dupe who'd ordered a veggie dog. "I wouldn't give you cocksuckers any protein."

"Excuse me?"

"I said, it's chock full of protein. That'll be four bucks."

Charlie loses another sale and curses the fates. Screw it.

If he'd known this was National Pervert Day, he'd never have agreed to look after Herman's hot-dog stand for him. Not only is Charlie totally unprepared physically (no bottled water, no veggie dogs), but also psychologically. For Charles "Charlie-boy" Jarvis is no sympathizer of the homosexual cause. Except in prison, which, as Charlie well knows, can turn anyone into a temporary shirt-lifter.

He's having a fearful time of it today, and not simply because he's been eating the profits and slagging the customers. Heck, he's lucky he hasn't caught AIDS serving all these homos. And if he has to hear another of these simpering, good-looking crimes against nature snap back with another fucking sausage joke he's going to ram it up their compromised immune systems.

To make matters worse, Charlie has the runs.

He scarfs back the butt-end of his umpteenth turkey sausage and wipes his hands on his Hawaiian shirt. Jeez, it's hot. Having to keep opening the cover of the barbie just adds to the blistering heat. He belches. He looks around. Wait a moment – where did all these people come from?

Something catches his eye. Feathers. Dark feathers glistening gold and green in the sun.

"Oh, shit."

Grabbing the meagre takings for the day and stuffing them into his pocket, Charlie hightails it over to the porta-potties before the crowd gets there. Nature calls.

Three hours later, the line for the porta-potties is one block long and three souls wide. An evil puddle seeps across the sidewalk, accompanied by a disconcerting chemical stench that hangs malevolently in the hot air.

Mrs. Adelaide Simcoe (sympathizer) is determined not to wet her Hush Puppies as she waits patiently in line. She castigates herself for lacking the foresight to relieve herself before the crowd hit. She'd had ample opportunity all morning, but she'd just sat at her table, unsuccessfully trying to hawk her mosaic lampstands. (They resemble toilet-brush holders, truth be told).

Then, when the crowd came, the chance of finally unloading some of her handicrafts outweighed her desire to urinate. She should have listened to her bladder. So far, she's managed to sell just one of her creations – and that was to her partner-in-crime and fellow stall-deposit holder: the ever-jaunty Phoebe Spadina (lesbian), so the sale doesn't really count.

It was Phoebe who'd talked her into this fiasco in the first place. They were good friends, having met a few years back at Adelaide's first group art show at the now-defunct *fugu* art gallery. This Gay Pride Proposition, as presented by Phoebe, had all sounded rather grand. Phoebe and friends would sell their art (which ended up being strange mobiles crafted from recycled cat-food cans), Adelaide would sell her mosaics and they'd all be gazillionaires by the end of the day – a gazillion dollars proving to be about 0.2 percent of a Hong Kong dollar, and that doesn't include the non-returnable deposit in the calculation.

Still, there're a few hours to go. It could get better. Except that Phoebe and her friend, Alexander Church (homosexual), dropped acid an hour ago, and neither has proved worthy company for the past twenty minutes.

A sweating girl to Adelaide's left is studying her Swiss wristwatch with one eye and the slow but inevitable progress of the porta-potty line with the other.

"At an average of three and a half minutes per visit," mutters this girl to no one in particular, "divided by the number of toilets, multiplied by the number of people ahead of us . . ."

Adelaide zones out and concentrates on her T'ai Chi breathing. If she successfully pretends to be made out of marble, she might make it to sundown before she explodes.

At her other elbow, there's a little man in a floral leotard, blond fright wig, high heels, and too much panstick, agonizingly shifting his weight from foot to foot. Determined to kill two birds with one stone, he's handing out flyers while he waits in line.

"Drop by later! Give me some immoral support."

Adelaide already has one of his flyers dutifully tucked into her raffia purse – a photocopied image of Hollywood celebrity look-alikes waving merrily from the centre of a starburst: *Hollywood Talent Contest! Top Prize* $100! Adelaide has no intention of going.

"Oooh," moans the poor man, squirming like Marilyn. "My pride can only take so much of this."

The line inches forward slowly. It's going to be a while.

There's a dark house on the other side of the park, shrouded with ivy, bitterness, death, and remorse. Its custodian, Olive Palmerston, won't be celebrating gay pride any time soon. There is nothing remotely gay or happy about Olive.

Oh, she has fresh garden flowers on her coffee table and a genteel smile on her face, but there's a wooden crucifix over her bed and enough pharmaceuticals in her fridge to level a field of elephants. For the past six years, Olive has been renting out her ground-floor room to the sick and dying – an arrangement that capitalizes on her earlier calling in life as a nurse. And nurses are angels. Thus, despite being unable to find any joy for herself on this homosexual holy day, Olive has enough martyred civility in her bones not to openly begrudge the happiness of others.

Right now, however, she stands seething with a confused anger before her upstairs closet, an empty hatbox gripped in her hands. The closet is where she keeps the sacred remnants and bequests of her lodgers. Clothing, photographs, jewellry – dozens of tragic memories all safely stored away in the dark. And now it appears that her collection has been raided. The feather boa is gone.

Donald must have taken it, Clarence couldn't possibly have made it up the stairs in his wheelchair. The nerve! And to think that she'd expressly forbidden it!

She remembers the conversation distinctly. No, they couldn't borrow the feather boa. No, not even if it was Clarence's last Gay Pride Day before he passed on, that wasn't the point. They could borrow the melon frock, some pantyhose and the sun hat with the linen daisies. But the feather boa had belonged to her brother, and regardless of Clarence's own proximity to death's door, she had refused to budge on the issue.

So that's what they'd been up to that morning, Clarence keeping her out in the garden admiring the chrysanthemums while Donald snuck upstairs to her closet. The scheming pansies.

Olive stifles a wave of indignation as her gaze settles on a thick-framed snapshot on her vanity. Her brother in happier days, his face surrounded by dark feathers. He seems to offer some consolation, if not company.

There, but for the grace of God . . .

Adelaide is finally at the front of the line. Canadian-Express-style, it has only taken a half-hour to reach this position of privilege. She's had her eye firmly fixed on the cubicle at the end of the row for the past ten minutes. No one has yet come out of it, or gone near it. Everyone's been playing goody-goody-swap-shoes, only entering a cubicle as someone exits. That end outhouse is empty. It's got to be. No one could stay in one of those things longer than five minutes.

Deciding not to wait for the next magical cabinet to vacate, Adelaide strides to the end of the row. Even if there is someone in there, she decides, she'll give 'em a rousing talking-to for taking up so much time. See? She was right. The little red *occupied* flag isn't even up. It says *vacant*. She yanks open the door.

Only it isn't vacant.

A fat hairy arm flops into Adelaide's face.

She begins to close the door, but is too late. A gaudy Hawaiian shirt blurs past her view, followed by something dark and feathery, patterned shorts and then – *thump-a-bonk* – the entire weight of a corpse lands at her Hush Puppies.

"Oh, pooh!"

Adelaide clamps her hand over her nostrils in reaction to the experimental laboratory aroma. He's dead. Very dead. Adelaide has had some experience with corpses; she knows one when she sees one, and they all look pretty much the same. Indeed, if her own husband wasn't currently residing in an urn on her kitchen window ledge between the pot scourer and the Mr. Bubbles, Adelaide might have thought (from the taste in leisure clothes alone) that this might be Wellington himself. Similar build, similar weight, similar gender. Dead.

These particular remains have been stewing in that hot-house for some time. The face is monstrous. Bloated. The eyes bulge, glazed over, a milky grey. All down the side of the puffy face there are purple blotches, and the tongue has swollen to the size of a small grapefruit in the open mouth. It looks like a pig's head on an Oktoberfest platter.

The cause is obvious: strangulation. One hand still clutches at the beautiful ostrich-and-peacock-feather boa that digs into the neck. It's an alluring accessory, if not entirely fetching in its current ensemble. Adelaide is aware of a crowd creeping up behind her.

"Whoa. That's one hell of a tie-off," says one.

"Looks like she's had too many poppers," says another. And so on.

"My boa!"

It's the leaflet-distributing transvestite in the floral leotard. His eyes glisten, birdlike, as he approaches the corpse. A tight, constrained half-smile through the panstick.

"Oh my God, it's my boa! I've been looking all over for it!"

And before Adelaide can stop him, the strange little man unravels the boa from its gruesome model, hugs it close to his faux bosom and vanishes into the crowd.

"The dead man is *who*?"

"Charles Jarvis. Recognize the name, Mrs. Simcoe?"

Adelaide feels grafted to her plastic chair. She stares at the clock on the police-station wall directly ahead of her and gives a little shudder, which turns into a little shake of her head. Charles Jarvis? Nope. Never heard of him. She isn't going to let Chief Inspector Parkway know the truth.

After all, he's been good enough to pretend he doesn't recognize *her*.

The Chief pushes a few files around his desk and continues: ". . . known as "Charlie-boy" to his friends. An habitual criminal, was our Charlie. Petty larceny, cigarette smuggling, wife beating, the usual. Always giving us the runaround, so I can't say I'm sorry to see him go. His wife's going to be darn pleased, too."

Adelaide nods involuntarily. From what she remembers of her brush with "Charlie-boy" Jarvis, she has to admit that she also has little problem with the concept of "dead Charlie."

"No shortage of suspects, then?" she asks.

"Suspects? What on earth for?"

"Well, I did find him strangled in the porta-potty."

The Chief puts down a pen. "With what was he strangled, Mrs. Simcoe?"

"With a feather boa."

"I didn't see any feather boa," smiles the Chief. "Looked like a heart attack to me. Brought on by suffocation. It gets awful hot in those mobile toilets, you know."

"So you're not going to . . . to investigate?"

The Chief closes a file folder and checks his watch. "Would you care to sign your statement now or later, Mrs. Simcoe?"

▼

"So it's like a locked room mystery?" asks Phoebe Spadina, unloading their unsold handicrafts from the back of the station wagon. "Cool."

"No," says Adelaide, rummaging through her purse. "The porta-potty was unlocked when I got there. Anyone could have gotten in. Now where did I put that flyer?"

"Oh." Phoebe plays with one of her cat-food-can mobiles distractedly. "What are you going to do?"

"What I always do, of course," snaps Adelaide, putting on her reading spectacles. "Investigate. Aha! Here it is. Hollywood Talent Contest. Ever been to Buzby's?"

▼

By ten o'clock that evening, Buzby's is packed. Adelaide and Phoebe sit at a table with a fair view of the stage. The lineup for the evening so far has included a drag queen, a drag queen, a drag queen, a drag queen who did the splits, and a drag queen. No sign as yet of the pansticked wonder who absconded with the feather boa.

"Did we have to come here?" complains Phoebe, stabbing her cocktail with a straw.

Adelaide ignores her and scans the crowd. Darn. They all look the same, these men in frocks. And the lighting doesn't help.

Three more sad lip-synching demonstrations slide by onstage.

▼

"It's what's left out," concludes Phoebe eventually. "That's where the art form lives."

Adelaide is about to agree when Edith Piaf steps into the spotlight.

"That's him!" she shouts, pointing to the creature wobbling on its heels. "And that's the feather boa!"

Non, rien de rien . . .

From the other side of the footlights, Lady Summer Magnolia is dying a thousand and one deaths of humiliation. She's overcome by the combination of a hostile audience, terror, fear, stolen feather boa, and various powders.

Her lips and neck have too much rigor, her smile is giving her a migraine. Her heart is pumping louder than the soundtrack (which she can't hear anyway through the wig), and the follow spot is a searchlight from Auschwitz.

She's missed her entrance, forgotten all the words to the song she once knew so well at three o'clock in the morning, and now she's about to be fingered for a murder she didn't commit.

"That's him!"

Lady Summer Magnolia soldiers bravely through her number, vaguely following a distant choreography. She can't keep her eyes off that ginger-haired woman.

"And that's the feather boa!"

The words shrivel her stomach. Oh, how she wishes she'd never swiped the feathered monstrosity now curling its way lasciviously around her throat! But she couldn't help it. It had been a compulsive act.

Je ne regrette rien . . .

In a flurry of powder, winking with its peacock eyes from amidst the black ostrich, the feather boa is shoved, suddenly, into Adelaide's lap.

It takes her a good ten seconds to realize what's happened. By that time Edith Piaf has abandoned the stage. Adelaide shakes her head in wonder, blinks a couple of times back at the boa, then smiles.

"It's off to forensics with you!"

Over on the other side of the park, in the ivy-covered house dedicated to death and remorse, Olive Palmerston pours a stiff drink for the grown man who sits weeping in her kitchen. Really. It's not as if Clarence's death was unexpected; he'd been hanging on by a T-cell for months.

And who gets to sort out the death certificate? Who gets to tidy up the mess in the bathroom? Who gets to sort through the personal effects? Who gets to play the same game again and again, tenant after tenant, until she finally gets over her brother's death six years ago?

"There you go, Don. That'll steady your nerves."

"I can't . . . I can't believe he's . . . I mean, he actually died on Pride Day," moans Donald, stroking the empty wheelchair. "It was . . ."

Olive nods sympathetically while her anger twists – hidden – inside. She wants to shake him by the shoulders and scream in his face. *What have you done with my feather boa*?! *You lousy thief*! But her professional nurse persona is too strong for such an out-burst. She'll save the issue of the boa for later, when it'll have the best effect.

". . . the excitement. That's what killed him." Donald takes another swig of the Glenmorangie single malt, oblivious to its pedigree. "In a way, I'm happy."

"So am I, Don." She realizes they're talking about completely different things. "So am I."

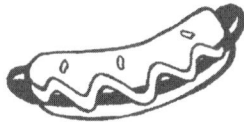

Adelaide Simcoe puts down the morning paper and takes a sip of coffee. She gazes out her kitchen window, lost in thought.

Three days after the event, the death of petty criminal Charles "Charlie-boy" Jarvis has managed to garner two inches of print on page sixteen, lost amongst titillating snippets of hookers and drug dealers. *Heart-Attack Charlie.*

No mention of being strangled to death by a particularly distinctive feather boa (swiped by the first passing drag queen), let alone being found in a porta-potty at Gay Pride Day.

There is, however, a small picture of him (front and profile) and the address where the funeral will be held later on that day. Now why would they print that? Could it be that a crowd is expected?

Adelaide picks up the murderous feather boa still encased in one of her extra-large freezer bags. It had been a simple matter to get it back from the thieving drag queen. But on Monday, it had proved impossible to have it examined by forensics without a case file number. Clearly, it's still up to her to get to the bottom of this mystery.

So the funeral is this afternoon? Hmm. Adelaide checks her watch and tries to remember where she put her funeral duds.

▼

In the dark, ivy-covered house on the other side of the park, Olive Palmerston is in her element. The potluck memorial service for Clarence Draper is of the stuff that makes her life worth living. She's smothered the front room in chrysanthemums, festooned the front door with black ribbons, and baked a dish of her ham-and-spinach lasagna.

The turnout is good: about three dozen. Mainly ex-colleagues from before Clarence got sick. Some are bravely sitting in the front room, listening to the Reverend sermonize. But most have escaped to the garden, where they wander in the sunshine with their loaded-up party plates in one hand and their photocopied program of the afternoon's schedule in the other.

Over by the apple trees, two fashionable young men openly flirt with each other while tossing scalloped potatoes to a bull-dog (which is welcome, but not inside the house). Their laughter tempers the sober gathering.

Donald Silverthorne, boyfriend to the recently demised, skulks in the shaded passageway by the garage, pretending to read and then not read the newspaper. He's been acting funny all day —

distant, preoccupied – and it's not just his bereavement, thinks Olive. No, he's got a guilty conscience. And well he should. It's time to let him know his treachery hasn't gone unnoticed.

"You may not have been one of my lodgers, Donald," she whispers, sidling up to him, ostensibly to hand him a sausage roll. "But if you lost my feather boa at the Gay Pride Parade, you're going to wish you were."

"I . . . I didn't touch it. I mean –"

"I've got my eye on you, Donald Silverthorne."

And with that, Olive leaves him to sink into the pit of his own misery and returns to her social garden. Fluttering conversations of regret and commiseration drift through the summer air as she winds her way back through the crowd as if dancing a stately Elizabethan pavane, adding a sympathetic word or two to her left, a practiced smile and a worldly shake of the head to her right.

It's the little things in life that bring the greatest pleasures.

The Necropolis looks as if it's been taken over by the Teamsters' annual picnic. Whole families in leisure wear, with the occasional off-duty policeman thrown in for slight variance. Charlie's funeral is clearly an event no one wants to miss.

The feather boa suits Adelaide the way her Hush Puppies would suit an erotic dancer. She feels uncomfortable, conspicuous and ostentatious, but she's determined to follow through on her hunch: that the murderer won't be able to resist putting in an appearance. The boa around her neck is the bait.

Suspects, suspects, suspects.

It doesn't take Adelaide long to learn that the cackling

woman in pink rayon, leaning against a headstone and knocking back margarita mix, is Charlie's new widow, Isabella. No reaction to the boa, however, no matter how much Adelaide primps and preens.

Then Adelaide insinuates herself into a conversation with a hulking lump of a man, Herman, who for some reason thinks she's Charlie's old grade-school teacher.

"The thing I can't figure out," muses Adelaide, "is what Charles was doing at Gay Pride in the first place."

"I sure tricked him good on that one, huh?" chuckles Herman. "I'd never have gotten him to look after my hot-dog stand if I'd told him about the poofters. And I told him to lay off those skanky turkey dogs."

Hot-dog stand? Charlie was selling hot dogs at Pride Day? Turkey dogs?

Adelaide clicks her tongue against the roof of her mouth. "It must have been *awful* for him," she says, eventually. "He must have suffered terribly."

▼

Olive Palmerston pays the taxi driver and clambers out at the wooden Gothic Revival porchway of the Necropolis. She feels giddy; things have happened so quickly. At the potluck memorial, someone had casually shown her a snapshot of Clarence in the parade *wearing her boa* and that had done it.

Crack!

In a fit of fury, she'd snatched the photo and gone screaming in search of Donald, who'd heard her coming and was already struggling to get his Honda started. Luckily, a cab was passing.

But what was he doing here at the Necropolis? Another funeral party?

She trudges up the concrete path under the hot sun, suddenly feeling stupid for chasing halfway across town on impulse. She spots Donald up ahead, creeping about, trying to hide behind his newspaper. He seems interested in a gaggle of people over by a particularly ancient obelisk.

Then Olive sees it, too. A middle-aged, ginger-haired woman, fluffing and preening around in . . .

"My boa!" Olive yells. "What's that woman doing with my feather boa!?"

Without thinking, she breaks into a run.

"Wheee!"

Adelaide Simcoe betrays her pleasure as she sails across University Avenue in hot pursuit of a powder blue Honda. Just missing a bicycle courier, she swerves, stalls, then waves merrily at her fellow motorists. The game is no longer afoot, it's now *à voiture*.

Her plan to entrap the murderer with the feather boa had worked better than expected. She'd been set upon by a screaming harridan who was, it appeared, the owner of the boa.

In the ensuing madness, a tug-of-war had developed beneath the wooden porch, and the boa had been swiped (yet again) by a gawky man who'd sprung out from behind a newspaper and who'd vanished in a Honda.

"Aha! There you are!" Adelaide spots her quarry up ahead turning towards Chinatown, barely keeping four wheels on the road. Throwing a quick prayer heavenwards, Adelaide cuts the corner a good twenty yards ahead of the intersection.

"Wheee!"

The early Wednesday evening drinking crowd on College is a combination of those just getting off work and those just trying to get off the patio since lunch. Alexander Church would normally belong to the latter group, but today he had an afternoon engagement and is only now just finishing his first drink. What's thrown him off schedule was a potluck memorial ceremony for a friend who'd died on Sunday and where, it must be said, he fell in love.

"Another beer, sexy?"

"Mmm."

Alex's pupils dilate as Murray's dreamy torso twists and hoists itself around to catch the attentions of the waiter. The best thing about Murray, thinks Alex, apart from the physique, is that he's from New Zealand and that he's a doctor. (Or was it a dentist?) He also comes complete with his own bulldog, Dixie, who's currently hitched to the patio railing, snuffling at passersby in the hopes, perhaps, of some more scalloped potatoes.

The drinks ordered, Murray gives Alex a seductive wink. A similar wink had led to an athletic tryst in the washroom half an hour ago (where Alex grazed his knuckles) and from then on in, it's been one *double entendre* up the back-end of another.

The symptoms of love are unmistakable. Alex's heart rate, blood pressure and self-delusion levels are all soaring. He tells himself not to blow this one, that this one (i.e. Murray) has serious potential, and that if he plays his cards right, he could be sitting pretty on a doctor's practice, so to speak. He could just scream.

"So what line of work are you in, sexy?"

"Huh?"

Alex is shocked from his reverie by a reminder of the awful truth. "Me? I'm . . . I'm between jobs, right now."

"I could give you something to be getting on with."

This hi-octane moment is upstaged by a pale blue Honda veering up the sidewalk ten yards away, its horn squawking like some epileptic duck. The car plows through garbage bags, then crunches gently into a mailbox.

"Holy moley!"

Heads turn. Some folks raise themselves from their seats.

"Omigod," says Alex, recognizing the driver. "It's Donald."

Adelaide turns onto College just in time to see the crash. It surprises her that calamity hasn't struck earlier. Negotiating Chinatown had been a veritable John Woo car chase, complete with cabbage leaves now stuck to her windshield where she'd grazed a produce stall.

She pulls over, gets out, slams the door. Enough of this nonsense.

Out in the open, and clearly panicked, the driver of the Honda darts paranoid glances around him as he clutches the infamous boa to his chest. His wobbling gaze finally lands upon Adelaide striding towards him. He makes to run, but a voice hails him from a nearby patio.

"Donald! Hey Donald, are you okay?"

The moment of indecision is enough to give Adelaide time to catch up.

"Hello. Donald, is it?" She extends a hand. "I'm Adelaide. Nothing broken, I hope?"

His eyes widen.

"Was it the turkey dog that did it, Donald?" she continues. "Did you have one of Charlie's rancid turkey dogs?"

"Turkey dog?" He turns whiter. "It was a tur . . . wha . . . what turkey dog?"

"Gay Pride Day?" Adelaide prompts. "Did you have a grievance with a hot-dog vendor?"

"It was Clarence!" blurts Donald. "His immune system couldn't take the . . . I mean, the bastard said it was a vegg . . . " His head jerks him into an involuntary silence.

Adelaide considers her options. She almost feels sorry for the poor chap. "Suppose you tell me where you were running off to in such a hurry." She glances at his damaged car. "Can I give you a ride somewhere?"

▼

"What's up, sexy?"

Alex's heartbeat is returning to normal. The honeymoon's over. Reality pokes its ugly head into the picture, and if Murray calls him "sexy" one more time, he's going to barf. Besides, Murray's poky apartment stinks of dog.

"Nothing's up, Murray," he says, pulling on his pants. "And my name's Alex, in case you've forgotten."

"Alex, right." Murray makes the attempt to carve the name into his subconscious, but it's too late. Alex has decided that the guy's a fraud. Everything about him is false, from the cheap dye job to the New Zealand accent. He's not even a doctor. He's a dogsitter.

"I've gotta go."

"Hang on a sec." Murray finds a scrap of paper and scribbles down his number.

Alex thrusts the trick receipt into his pocket. He knows he won't call.

"Talk to you soon, then?" asks Murray, hopefully, giving Alex another one of his annoying smirks.

"Sure." Which, above and beyond being an out-and-out lie, isn't quite what he wants to say.

What Alex wants to say, as he leaves the apartment, as he leaves another toad kissing the dust behind him, is something more along the lines of, "Do you have something in your eye, Murray?"

He is, however, polite enough not to slam the door.

Sunlight splatters through the trees in the park, creating mottled shadows of sylvan delight as afternoon moves toward dusk. There is the scent of evening bonfires from nearby city garden lots. Adelaide Simcoe sits on a bench atop a hillock, calmly enjoying nature. She's quite chuffed with herself. She's solved a murder, had a car chase to boot, and is now putting the universe to rights under a well-earned sunset.

Her companion, however, is less than happy. Donald Silverthorne may as well be roasting in perdition. He rocks back and forth, clutching a bottle of lighter fluid. Every sweated move is awkward, every breath is tortured.

"Clarence didn't *mean* to strangle him," he grunts. "He was . . . Clarence was so angry after paying four bucks for a rancid veggie dog, and the feather boa was just *there*. I mean, I'd have thought it would have snapped before anyone got really hurt."

"It had a rubber core," mutters Adelaide, watching a plume of smoke curl above the trees. "A most effective tourniquet."

"And now Clarence is gone, too." Donald shakes his head, sadly. "The shock to his stomach from that street sausage was the final nail in his coffin. I mean, if he had a coffin. His ashes are scattered down there, you know."

"Yes. You told me."

Out of an instantly manufactured respect for the dead, they dutifully gaze at the group of elms beyond the beanpoles of the city allotments. A calm descends. A column of smoke rises. For a moment, everything seems at peace.

"Are you . . . are you going to tell the police?"

Adelaide shrugs. The police? They aren't particularly interested in catching Charlie's murderer, she knows that much. If anything, they'd probably cite Clarence for a posthumous award. If, indeed, it was Clarence who'd done the dirty deed.

"Tell me," she asks carefully, "how did Clarence get enough strength to strangle Charlie Jarvis? If he was as sick as you say he was, that is. And how did he get his wheelchair in and out of the porta-potty? You did say he was in a wheelchair, didn't you? I'm curious."

Donald looks offended, as if the answer to the question is obvious.

"Oh, didn't I tell you?" His face is the picture of innocence. "I did it for him."

Olive Palmerston is stunned. She's too late. Her beloved ostrich-and-peacock-feather boa has been dragged half-way across and back again from H-E-*double-hockey-sticks*, draped around foreign necks at festivals and funerals, tugged at, screamed over, stolen, abused every which way but Sunday, and now lies smouldering in a stinking heap at the foot of a bunch of elm trees in the park.

She'd guessed that Donald would come here – to the place where he'd scattered Clarence's ashes, where the two men had met, years ago. But what she couldn't have guessed was that he'd torch her precious boa as some kind of weird symbolic gesture. It's too much.

She pokes the still-smoking remains with her patent leather shoe. It looks like the cast-off skin of a snake coiled in the grass and weeds. The smell of burning rubber reminds her of a junkyard.

Her brother's treasured speckled feather boa. Kaput. Six years keeping it safe in the upstairs closet and now look at it. She feels

GREG

KRAMER

as if she's betrayed the family. As if she's betrayed every tenant who travelled through her front room on their way to the grave.

And yet in some strange way, she feels liberated. A burden has been finally lifted from her shoulders. Perhaps it's time to stop this morbid fascination.

Dusk turns to evening. Evening turns to night. Olive Palmerston walks home.

▼

"He died of *what*?!"

"Botulism, Mrs. Simcoe. Complicated by a heart attack and the lack of oxygen in the porta-potty." Chief Inspector Parkway hands Adelaide a sheet of paper. "So you can forget all about your grandiose strangulation and locked-room theories, if you don't mind."

"I never said . . ." Adelaide glances at the sheet, not wanting to rummage in her purse for her spectacles. "What's this? The autopsy report?"

"No. It's your statement. You forgot to sign it."

"Hmmph."

The Chief hands her a pen.

▼

Alexander Church sits stewing on the edge of his bed. He keeps catching his reflection in the mirror, but the angles aren't that good from where he is, and it's like trying to catch a ghost. He's descending into one of his dark moods again, and Lord knows, that could mean months before he's fit company.

He feels ugly. Old. Lazy.

He fiddles with a piece of paper. Murray's phone number,

rescued from the abyss of his jeans' pocket, salvaged just before the laundry. He stares at the firm, manly handwriting. Perhaps he'd been too tough on the guy. After all, who doesn't sometimes try a bit too hard to make a good impression on a first date? And Murray had seemed so perfect: sexy, employed, exotic.

Should he call? Shit. Alex curses himself that he's never been much for making executive decisions.

Murray had lied. He'd said he was a doctor (or was it a dentist?) when in reality he was nothing but a dogsitter. Lies.

In a fit of pique, Alex wads the paper into a tiny ball and flicks it into the corner of his room. The black mood has gotten the better of him.

"Fuck it."

"But why did you let him burn the feather boa? Wasn't it evidence?"

Phoebe Spadina stirs the ice cubes at the bottom of her glass while Adelaide sips gently on her Rusty Nail.

"Precisely," replies Adelaide, finally. "Evidence. I hate to admit it, but I couldn't sit by and see Charlie Jarvis's killer brought to justice."

Phoebe puts down her drink and grins at Adelaide. "Mrs. Simcoe, I do believe you're getting radical in your old age."

Adelaide scoffs and gestures towards the stage, where a drag queen in chunky running shoes bounds front and centre.

"Oh look!" she says, excitedly. "It's the one who does the splits."

the betrayal of rubber

(A Dental Romance)

Alexander Church's evil mood has settled in with a vengeance. Since the man of his dreams (solvent, good looking) is not forthcoming, then darkness must needs prevail. For two complete months, not one speck of daylight has penetrated his bachelor apartment. The blinds are permanently shut, the television permanently on. It's a black hole of stagnant compulsion – not so much an escape from his depression as a prison of suffocating self-loathing. A character flaw inherited from his parents, perhaps.

Empty bottles of Wild Turkey circle the bed, along with chip packets, porn videos, magazines and ashtrays. Occasionally, a fly buzzes in the gloom – *buzz, buzz, buzz* – around the lube-encrusted pile of tricks' phone numbers that accumulate in the corner.

The less said about certain dogsitters from New Zealand, the better.

The phone rings. Twelve times. A groan comes from the bed.

Alexander Church, the cause of all this detritus, lies half-naked in a comatose drunken slumber. He looks like a sailor washed up on some seaweed-strewn coastline, and stinks much like one, too. His legs are tangled in the sheets, an arm languishes off the edge of the mattress. Last night he'd announced to the room: "There's no satisfaction to be gleaned from this!" Then crashed out cold.

Clearly, it's time to snap out of it.

But Alex is waiting for an Omen from God before he'll dredge himself out of his personal mire. Since leaving home seven years ago, he's gone through one of these alcoholic funks annually. Like some tenacious virus, it plays itself out until either he gets sick of it, or it of him.

The phone continues to ring. A hand surfaces from the unconscious depths, gropes its way around the edge of the bed.

"Hnnn?"

"Alexander Church?"

"Nngh."

"Hi, Alex. This is Doctor Runnymede's office. You're due for your six-month checkup and cleaning. Would you care to make an appointment?"

▼

Cherry Beach's Rules for Modern Living, Number 82: Other people's sexual proclivities (no matter how exotic your own) can ruin your beauty rest. Case in point: Roxana's enigmatic visitor, currently whelping away in the boudoir to the lashings of a whip. The first half hour was entertaining. Now it's like a dripping tap.

Whoever heard of having sex in the middle of the day when some people are trying to sleep?

Cherry punches the divan cushions in an attempt to create a soft and downy pillow for her head. Fat chance. The divan is made of a stiff tapestry, a heavy-gauge sandpaper that threatens to shave the stubble from her dreams, should she ever succumb to the z's. It's also too short, so that her ankles, dangling off the end, fall asleep before the rest of her. It's been five weeks on this Procrustean bed, and she's still telling herself she'll get used to it.

Frustrated, Cherry pulls out her candy box of pills from one of her bags. Where's that elusive little blue marvel gone? The one that'll banish her into the Land of Nod – guaranteed – in twenty minutes or less. There's one left, she's sure of it.

As she searches, she keeps thinking that there must be easier (and quieter) ways for Roxana to earn a living, but realizes that there are probably none quite as expedient nor as lucrative. Roxana has a healthy clientele willing to pay by the welt for a little lunchtime discipline. So who is Cherry to complain?

"Aha! There you are!"

Cherry downs the pill with practiced ease and snuggles herself back onto the rigorous divan. Happily medicated, her mind starts running down the thousand and one sofas, foldouts, foamies, futons, and other temporary sleeping arrangements she's known in her haphazard life.

Others may count sheep. Cherry Beach counts couches.

"Feeling anything yet?"

From behind the dark glasses, the earphones, the nitrous

oxide mask, a rubber wedge jammed between his molars, the anaesthetic spreading through his gums, and the slurping tube in his gullet, Alex shakes his head. He doesn't know if he can feel anything or not. All he knows is that he wants Dr. Runnymede to fix him up. Slap him together.

The routine cleaning had revealed a couple of cavities that need attention. And although the cavity in his soul can't be mended with a simple amalgam, Alex hopes that subjecting himself to the dentist's chair might instigate an epiphany.

But so far, he hasn't even felt the needle.

Doctor Vernon Runnymede is the kind of dentist who puts his profession to shame. He's a friendly, bouncy man in his fifties, who can't abide any of his patients ever experiencing pain. He wears rainbow-framed spectacles and powder blue rubber gloves. Worse, he's efficient and compassionate.

"Hold tight and let me know if this hurts, okay?"

As the first strike of the drill approaches his gaping mouth, Alex feels the warm presence of Dr. Runnymede's hitherto unseen assistant two inches from his left ear. The hairs on his neck stand on end. His heart flutters.

He squints sideways to get a better peek.

Woh.

When they talk of love at first sight, surely they don't mean from behind multi-sensorial blindfolds? Alex can hardly believe his luck, but there it is: the dental assistant. Sparkly eyed. Blond (obviously bleached, but that's the way Alex likes 'em). And totally, totally humpy. Well, what he can see of him.

"I'm sorry, did that hurt?"

"Ng-hnh."

"Let's stop for a while then, and give the freezing some more time to kick in."

The epitome of discretion, Dr. Runnymede retreats from the room. Alex removes his encumbrances: the glasses, the nitrous mask, the earphones. He swivels round for a fuller inspection of his quarry.

"Hi, there."

No doubt about it: the guy in the scrubs is a dream. Those gorgeous eyes above the paper face mask twinkle with erotic promise. Was that a wink? Holding the gaze and feeling the thrill of the moment, Alex reaches out to touch a manly, tanned arm . . .

"You okay, mate?"

Alex's heart droops. He recognizes that voice. Those excruciating vowel sounds, that New Zealand lilt.

Murray.

"You!" Alexander Church sits up in the dentist's chair, glaring. "What are you doing here? You're supposed to be a dog-sitter, not a dental assistant!"

Murray reaches for the nitrous mask. "Here, give me a hit."

"What? Hey! I'm paying for that!"

Murray waves away argument as Alex collapses back in the chair. It's too much, he thinks. Here he is, dredging himself out of a two-month black-mood binge and who's the first person he bumps into? Nay, is attracted to? The pretentious heartthrob who'd precipitated it all in the first place. The sexy-as-all-heck bastard currently whoring back the nitrous.

"I hate my life."

Pertinent rundown of Alexander Church's Life: GWM, 27, 5'9", 160 lbs, blond hot guy downtown looking for similar. Subject to evil moods that can last months, cost a fortune, and require an Omen from God to end.

Alex hoists himself around to face Murray, an ultimatum on his mind. "Okay, I give up. You started this, so I guess you'd better finish it."

Murray stops, puzzled, the hissing gas halfway to his face. Shrugs. Smiles. "I get off at six."

When a woozy Cherry Beach tells a tipsy Handsome Jack that his favourite playmate, Mistress Roxana, is busy for the afternoon, she doesn't expect Jack to give her the once-over and ask if she's available instead.

"Well, actually," says Cherry in her best airline announcer's voice, "I'm only staying here for a couple of weeks while I sort myself out."

"You'll do."

Frightening words. Handsome Jack has that forthright way about him. A gambler's experience manifested in a rugged face, gently mottled with booze. His suit jacket hangs rakishly from his shoulders as he jingles the coins in his pocket. After a moment's thought he yanks out his wallet and waves a fistful of twenties under Cherry's nose, forcing a decision.

"You'd better come in," she yawns.

The pin money is running low of late, she has to admit, and the compensation for ruining her spine by crashing on Roxana's divan could well equal the bills in Jack's paw.

"Sit down." Cherry lights a cigarette before adding, brusquely, "like a good boy."

Jack perches himself on the edge of the hated divan.

"Do you do the rubber?" he asks.

Cherry knows enough that he isn't talking condoms. He's talking the asphyxiating Catwoman outfit Roxana has hanging in her closet. Frankly, at this time of day, Cherry would rather stick her head in a hot-water bottle, wrap herself in cling film and throw herself down the stairs. She drags on her smoke.

"Hard morning at the office?"

Jack shakes his head, produces a silver flask and offers it to her. "Vacation," he mumbles. "Three-day vacation."

Bender, thinks Cherry. Three-day bender. Still, she takes a swig of the proffered concoction.

"I could show you a little trick that'll make you feel ten years younger," she drawls.

She opens the door to Roxana's boudoir and steps into the shag-piled, nylon-swagged, vinyl-padded enclave. She waltzes over to the million-dollar closet as Roxana's parting words ring through her head.

"I'm going out. Hold the fort. Don't answer the phone. And keep out of my room."

It's early Friday evening and the Sisters of Avalon (formerly LaB-MAP – Lesbian and Bisexual Mothers with Alcoholic Partners) have taken over the Legion backroom. There is a scattering of middle-aged women and a couple of young 'uns, sharing their confessions of domestic horror in a vague, twelve-step kinda way.

Right now, there's one of those eternal silences. Judy, sitting at the glossy literature table, runs her hand over her coif, her ciga-rette dangerously close to the scratchy lacquer. If the whole thing were to catch, she would look much the same. A halo of pale blue flames around her head. A permanent look of astonishment.

This is her 368th meeting; she's an old hand. She's seen the Sisters of Avalon emerge from a splinter-hybrid group of Gay Moms 'n' Dads and AA, through chrysalis stages of Dykes With Kids, L-MAP, LaB-MAP, GaLaB-MaDwAP and a veritable alphabet of acronyms attempting to define their collective neurosis, depending on who's in the group at the time.

When things get bad Judy can always be counted on to break out in song. Something religious and stirring – a remnant from her East Coast chapel upbringing. Judy sings because today, as for the past seven years, she has nothing to report, nothing to confess. She's divorced her problem, solved her alcohol dependency, and the kids have both flown the nest. She doesn't have a girlfriend right now, true, but she has her television, her job in the Personnel Department of a downtown law firm. And this group.

Dare she make something up?

She could say that her dog of an ex-husband paid her a visit on one of his three-day benders. Smashed, say, three glasses and a window before passing out in the garage. That would be just like Jack. She can imagine every last detail as if it really had been last night instead of seven years ago.

Participants shift in their folding chairs, some look around the room. Okay, then. Judy clears her throat and starts singing in her scratchy mezzo.

"Fight the good fight wi-ith all thy might . . ."

"You looked at my file? How could you!"

"It's my job." Murray shrugs as they stroll through the park. "I always look over a file, just in case."

"Just in case of what?" Alex stops in his tracks.

"He-ey there." Murray seems genuinely cool. "It doesn't make any difference to me, mate."

"So where are we going?"

Adroitly sidestepping the issue, Alex twists the conversation into a debate over destination. His place is a bit of a mess, he maintains, while Murray's digs are "overrun with critters."

"Still dogsitting, then?"

Murray nods. "Three Yorkshire Terriers right now. You can help me walk them if you like."

Alex looks over to the dog exercise area where a crowd of owners just getting off work socializes. He feels the pressures of married life descend upon him.

"I don't believe in monogamy," he mumbles through the fading anaesthetic in his jaw.

But Murray, striding ahead and whistling a tuneless melody, doesn't hear. Alex follows, begrudgingly, a sickening sense of futility pulling at his groin.

This could be a big mistake.

GREG KRAMER

There's no hiding the crime: Roxana's fifteen hundred dollar all-in-one rubber suit that Cherry recently "borrowed" for an hour's session with Handsome Jack is now stretched in places it never was before.

"I could kill you, Cherry Beach," snarls Roxana, "if I thought it would make any difference."

"Perhaps you left it on the radiator by mistake?" offers Cherry, adrift in a sea of innocence. "They don't make those things like they used to, huh?"

Roxana slumps onto the divan, pushes Cherry's bags rudely out of the way and mumbles something about cuckoos in the nest, parasites that live on the couch and the possibility of the police being called in to oust a certain post-gendered omni-vestite from her life. Then her frustrated anger becomes too strong for her to stay in one place. She steams into the kitchen to fix herself a cocktail.

"They should put a label in those damned things," yells Cherry after Roxana's retreating swish. "How was I to know I was putting it on backwards!"

Silence. Guilt hovers around Cherry's eyelashes for a fraction of a second before vanishing in a couple of flutters.

What to do? She could brave it out here for a few more days before it either turns ugly or descends into a stagnant mire of inactive vitriol. Or she could get on the phone and canvass the community for a new couch.

Then again, she could give Handsome Jack a call. *Chickadee Vacations Inc.* That's what his business card, now tucked in her purse, says. She'd swiped it from his wallet along with a fifty-dollar tip. It wasn't stealing; he was right there when it happened. He'd called her a thieving bitch, which she'd taken as a compliment. The whole thing had degenerated into a fight over the keys to his Oldsmobile. What a joker that Handsome Jack was!

The sweet music of Roxana playing with the kitchen knives wafts into the room. Decision made. Cherry gathers her bags.

"It's no good, mate. It's not happening for me."

Murray sits on the edge of the bed and glares at the rain pouring down outside. Beside him, Alex buckles his belt, zips up his jeans. Shit. What had started off as an energetic grapple o' the glutei has ended up as a hiatus of impotency. It was their third bash at the can in two days, each time with the same result: *coitus collapso.*

It's my damned file, thinks Alex. Murray snuck a look at it in the dental office and the virus has now spread off the page and into their bed, developing into an invisible, unspoken condition that's emptied the lead from their pencils.

"It's not you," says Murray, "it's me. I'm sorry."

"Yeah, right," mutters Alex. "You and your ability to read my file, perhaps?"

A fly lands on the neck of a Wild Turkey bottle, where it hides, motionless, in a shadow. Alex flicks it away. He wants to inquire after Murray's own health, whether he even knows his status. He decides he doesn't care.

"Screw you," he snaps.

"Would if I could, mate." Murray sighs. "Look Alex, latex makes my johnny go numb, if you must know."

"We hadn't even got to the condom stage," Alex reminds him.

"But what if we had!"

"And what if we'd been struck by lightning?"

"Well, excuse me, buster, but in a way you have!"

Alex glares. That was below the belt. So he was one of the "unclean" now, was he? One of the untouchables? His eyes wander around the filth of his bachelor pad. The empty bottles, the dirty laundry. Murray, red-faced, in the middle of it all. The mess of his life. "Struck by lightning?" He grabs his jean jacket and makes for the door. "I didn't realize it was a competition to see who lives the longest!"

Alex gives the door a satisfying slam on his way out. He strides down the hallway, clipping the walls with his fist as he goes. When he gets out on the rainy sidewalk he kicks a tree. Damn.

▼

Chickadee Vacations Inc. is in one of the tallest office towers in the city, on the sixty-eighth floor. One storey away from debauchery, thinks Cherry, as the elevator rips its high-speed journey up the centre of the building. She grins primly at her fellow business-class frequent flyers and gathers her four large garbage bags of belongings closer. In her haste, she's forgotten to dress for the occasion. Typical. She gets out, her ears ringing with embarrassment.

At the anonymous reception desk she flashes Handsome Jack's business card.

What a view from the picture windows! From this height, a fallen woman such as herself could make quite an impression in the world.

"He's in 29D, which is down to your right, through the photo-copying room, kitty corner to the coffee machines, third opening to your left, next to the washrooms."

"Huh?"

The receptionist flourishes a photocopied sheet. "Would you care for a floor plan?"

Cherry gratefully takes the map and sets off to find the Lost City of Chickadee Vacations. Within seconds, the panoramic view of the city has gone and she's wandering around in a windowless maze, causing her to think that perhaps the whole building is a sham – a cityscape projected onto screens and in reality she's deep underground.

Eventually, after a few collisions with bustling secretaries, she finds 29D. It's not much bigger than a broom closet.

Handsome Jack snoozes with his feet up on a desk amid boxes of travel brochures. Like a dozing tomcat on the lookout, he cracks an eye as Cherry enters the tiny room.

"What are you doing here?" His face is haggard.

"I tried calling," she lies, "but I couldn't get through."

She swings her bags into a pileup at the corner of the desk. She meets Jack's bewildered stare with a toothy smile.

"I decided to take you up on your offer." She flips her pageboy wig, flashing her earrings. "Don't worry. I can sleep in the car."

Summer has turned. The days are sharper, the nights dull. The fireworks are over, construction is stuttering towards completion and the city hauls itself in from off the patio and opens the sweater drawer.

"We plow the fields and sca-atter . . ."

Judy Church sews another sequin onto the pantsuit, a song in every stitch. This year she's going as Elvis, along with all the gals from group. Yes, there'd been an argument, but all those coming with the Sisters Of Avalon were coming as Elvis, and those who weren't, weren't.

She's looking forward to the party. Halloween is as exciting as Christmas once was for her as a kid.

"The good seed on the la-and . . ."

Judy belongs to a modern family. She divorced her gamblin', boozin' husband at the same time she came out of the closet, taking the cue from her gay son, who she hasn't seen in years. These days, her family consists of the lesbian mothers support group, the Sisters Of Avalon. And a very fine family it is, too. They meet weekly and, as a group of ten or more, get discounts on all kinds of events – from demolition derbies to day trips to the Black Gulch Pioneer Settlement. That kind of privilege was never extended to her blood family. Size, in this day and age, clearly counts.

Judy bites through some cotton thread and adjusts her thimble as if it were a wedding ring. Halloween. What fun. She casts her eye to the envelope resting on her mantelpiece. Inside is her ticket for the Halloween Ball at the AMORQ Temple: $15 a head instead of the $25 for the ordinary, everyday homosexual.

She threads another sequin onto her needle. Only three more outfits to go after this one.

"By God's almighty ha-and . . ."

Cherry Beach is working the slots. Perched on a stool, she shoves token after token into the greedy machine, smoking herself into a stupor and occasionally winning a spittle of coin. Handsome Jack's over at the track, feeding his own addiction. What a couple they make!

For nigh on seven weeks now, Cherry has been living in the back seat of Jack's Oldsmobile in return for favours in the bedroom. Three or four times a week she dons the rubber and exercises her skills with the bullwhips and cat-o'-nine-tails.

"Chickadee!"

Cherry looks up from the one-armed bandit as Jack arrives out of breath, his loose change jangling in his pocket.

"Chickadee, look!" he exclaims, brandishing a fistful of bills. "Twenty-five to one!"

Oh yay, thinks Cherry. More money to spend on frivolities.

"My, that's a lot of cash for a young lad like you to be carrying around." She casually opens her Cadillac purse, its dark mouth yawning in Jack's direction. "Don't forget to feed the baby."

▼

Liberty Hanna could never in a thousand years be described as conservative. Her penchant for black leather, tattoos, skull rings, things punk, shaved heads, and body piercings is far too embedded in her psyche.

But the reflection in her mirror speaks otherwise: pink stockings, a mauve dress with frills aplenty, and a golden wig back-combed into a stiff cockerel's pompadour. She needs to find some smart pumps to replace her steel-toed boots, but other than that (and a dash of makeup) she's the picture of sugar-gloss girlie-girl.

"Ugh! I look horrific!"

Which is the desired effect of any Halloween costume worth its salt.

This particular outfit has to serve an extra duty. Since last year's debacle at the Temple (involving flooded washrooms and spray paint), Liberty is barred for the next three thousand years.

Screw them. She has her $25 ticket, she has her disguise. That should be enough to get her through the doors, no problem.

Once inside, it'll be even easier to keep clear of the bouncers and security who all know her name better than their own. The AMORQ Temple is huge. It holds two thousand (legally) and covers four levels, six dance floors, seven balconies and a secret room behind the Great Egyptian Chamber. As long as she doesn't overindulge with her glue bag, she should be fine.

Besides, this year, her drug of choice is Special K. Less stink. She has five vials put aside for the big night. Well, four and a bit.

She taps out a little pyramid of powder onto the back of her hand. She adds a tap more for good measure. Then a bit more. Finally, she snorts back enough veterinary-grade ketamine to stun a small cow.

"Scrambled tofu!"

Liberty Hanna's over-pink reflection in the mirror starts to melt as the drugs hit her brain.

The place is clean. Unbelievable. Alexander Church blinks twice and wonders if he's accidentally walked into the wrong bachelor apartment.

Someone has been in, done the dishes, the laundry, vacuuming, everything. Midnight elves?

Or could it be a certain dental-assistant-cum-dogsitter from New Zealand who is the only one (apart from the superintendent) with a spare set of keys? Hah!

Alex's first reaction is amazement, followed shortly by anger. Just because they're spending two nights a week with each other is no excuse. How dare he! Then, when he spots the beribboned bottle of Wild Turkey on the bed, his antagonism melts. He pours himself a drink.

There are fresh-cut flowers in a vase. The whole place smells of summer.

He reaches for the phone, punches in a number from memory and is answered on the first ring.

"Room service, can I help you?"

Oh ha-ha, thinks Alex. Call display.

"Hi, Murray," he says aloud in a singsong voice. "You've been busy, I see."

GREG KRAMER

"Are you pissed at me?

Alex searches under the bed with one hand. "No-o," he says. "No, I'm not pissed. Not yet. What have you done with the condoms?"

Silence on the other end. Then: "I didn't realize we'd reached the condom stage."

"Ready when you are, Batman," quips Alex.

"Okey-dokey." Murray sounds like a man on a mission. "Don't move. I'll be right over."

The line goes dead. Alex slams the receiver onto the cradle.

"Presumptuous bastard!"

He stares into his drink. Shit. He should have gotten the asshole to bring over some ice.

By some sleight o' fate, the AMORQ Temple was deconsecrated in the sixties. Certain Masonic sculptures were removed from the Great Egyptian Chamber, while the basement was hurriedly done over with concrete. Since then, thirty years of rock concerts, parties, rentals, functions, and sometimes merely standing empty twiddling its arcane rosewood carvings have done little to detract from the Temple's grandeur. It's an imposing building; a marvel of interior design; an ornate sanctuary in the heart of the city.

Tonight, in keeping with its mystic roots, it plays host to a Halloween Ball. A healthy crowd of assorted gremlins, vampires, and creatures from the Black Lagoon haunt the premises, bumping and grinding into the night. The competition for best costume isn't for another half-hour. If there's any justice in the world, the building should win the prize, hands down.

The place is an obstacle course. Gravestones, junkyard debris, old cars, twisted trees, and Gothic arches litter the dance floor like giant chess pieces. Stuffed owls and vultures lurk amongst ivy and cobwebs. The lighting – all flashes and strobes – is downright dangerous. The dry ice doesn't help.

Throughout this scenic profusion, drag queens cavort with goblins, Roman slaves with serial killers, ghouls with ghouls, and Borgias with Karloffs. A coven of Elvis Presley drag kings saunters through the wreckage, jokingly shaking its collective hip and breaking out into "Blue Suede Shoes" at the slightest provocation. Something that looks like a giant snail glides by, its operator belly down on a skateboard, a trail of Mylar glistening in its wake. Halloween merriment.

Trick or Treat!

"Here's your number. Don't wander too far, the judging's in half an hour."

In the not-so-secret alcove behind the Great Egyptian Chamber, Liberty Hanna, uncomfortable in mauve secretary dress, blond wig, pink stockings, and pumps, finds herself in line for the costume competition. She hadn't intended on entering, she'd just ducked into the shadows to give herself another super-bump of Special K, and the damned lineup just formed around her. If they find her, they'll toss her out, no questions asked. But no one would ever think this pink and frothy monstrosity was the notorious Liberty Hanna. Only a sharp observer might notice Liberty's indisputable identifying mark: the missing middle finger of her right hand.

The security guard handing out the numbers scowls at the dozen or so drag Elvis Presleys. "OK, so let me get this straight," he barks. "You all want to enter as one contestant?"

General agreement. An Elvis in the back starts to sing, but is shushed by her companions.

Right then. One contestant it is.

"Next?"

Liberty suddenly finds herself at the front of the line.

"Who are you supposed to be, then?"

"Bubblegum zombie," gurgles Liberty, as ketamine drips down the back of her throat.

"Right you are, then," he yawns. Clearly, this guy doesn't think much of her costume. He scribbles something down on his clipboard and hands over number 54.

With her right hand, Liberty reaches out to grasp the numbered plastic disc, and immediately realizes her undoing. She succumbs to a wave of slow-motion nausea.

Fuck it. She's betrayed herself.

The security guard stares at Liberty's fingerstub as if recalling a time gone by. His eyes narrow, accusingly.

"Hey! Don't I know you? Wait! Come back!"

Like the proud owner of a pedigree Rottweiler, Cherry Beach parades Handsome Jack around the corridors of the AMORQ Temple. As Ilse, Queen of the Nazis, Cherry wears her stainless steel stiletto heels, while Jack is on all fours beside her. Bound and gagged from head to tail in bright red latex, he depends on Cherry's leadership skills to prevent him from banging into walls. He can hear well enough, thanks to the earflaps, so she's directing him with a series of tugs on the leash, finger snaps and low, almost inaudible commands.

"To your right . . . there you go. OK. Good boy."

Handsome Jack is enjoying every grovelling moment of it, Cherry can tell. She has to remove his hood to get a drink to his mouth, and going to the washroom is a fifteen-minute ordeal. But other than these minor fantasy spoilers, the two of them are happy as a set of thumbscrews.

Rounding a corner to the rear of the Great Egyptian Chamber, they bump into a crowd of Elvis Presleys. A dozen of them in their spangled suits.

"Heel!"

"Woah, gals," drawls an Elvis. "Look what we have here: Lassie in rubber!"

"Does he know any tricks?"

Never one to resist an appreciative audience, Cherry runs Jack through his paces. She gets him to beg, roll over, goose step, salute and – as a finale – lick his balls, which he doesn't quite manage without toppling over.

"Bravo!"

The Elvi know true entertainment when they see it.

"Give him a bone!"

"Oh, I assure you, he's already got one," laughs Cherry. "Better get the poor sod a drink!"

▼

"Who are you supposed to be, then?" asks the taxi driver, pulling up outside the Temple. "No, don't tell me. Tallulah Bankhead, right? Right?"

Alex pouts and fingers his pearls. He hates keeners.

"You look like Tallulah Bankhead," continues the cabbie. "And so does your buddy."

"That's right, mate," says Murray, paying the fare. "We're both Tallulahs. Two for one. Keep the change."

Alex stares out of the window and lets his vision blur. It's raining – a gentle splatter of multicoloured drops on the window reflects the slick street outside. He feels mischievous.

They clamber out of the cab, each clutching a bag of popcorn to his superflat chest. They are identical, from their wigs to their shoes. Twin twin-sets.

"Shit, look at that lineup. You got the tickets, Murray?"

"Dah-ling," comes the arch reply. "Who do you take me for?"

That's enough to start a minor popcorn fight as they converge upon the Temple entrance.

It had been a stroke of genius, thinks Alex, to both go as Tallulah. They'd gotten the inspiration the previous week while watching *Eyes Of A Stranger*. The scene in the park where Ms Bankhead scatters popcorn to the pigeons was the clincher.

"What could possibly happen to me here with my little . . . chaperones!" shrieks Alex, tossing his ticket and a few kernels of popcorn to the dragon lady in the box office. "Shit, these mushrooms are strong!"

"They're poison, Alex!" belches Murray. "The bloody things are poisonous!"

With faces of immobile rock, the bouncers with their radio earsets wave them through the once-sacred Temple doors. The evening awaits.

▼

Up in one of the balconies, Liberty Hanna catches her breath. She's managed to give the security guys the slip. A wonder-warp of ketamine has helped rather than hindered her escape. She's been scampering in and out of stairwells, dance floors, washrooms, and at least fifteen galactic dimensions to reach safety. Naturally, she's a tad winded.

Steadying herself against the wall, she taps out another mammoth toot of ketamine onto the back of her hand. Honk. That's better.

"There she is!"

"Get her!"

Bugger it. Caught in the grip of a humongous K-hole, Liberty's eyes wobble in their sockets. Somewhere to her right she spots a dance floor, the party-goers small and distorted, as if seen through the wrong end of a telescope.

There is no time, however, to ponder the wonders of hallucinogens. She has to get away. And the dance floor is as good a place as any to get lost amongst the throng of Halloween goblins.

Like a bull about to charge, Liberty lowers her head in an attempt to sharpen her focus. Her target is the approximate centre of writhing and jiving humanity. Following this logic, she hikes her dress, hoists a pink-shod foot onto the brass rail at the edge of the dance floor (now where did that come from?), and launches herself into the Great Egyptian Chamber.

Oops. Wasn't she up in the balcony?

"Scrambled fucking tofu!"

▼

"Heads up!"

Carrying a piña colada above her head through the crowd, Judy Church comes to the conclusion that she's having a hoot. From the moment she donned her sequined pantsuit, she knew that tonight was going to be a success. Twelve further members of the Sisters of Avalon decided to brave their insecurities and don the Elvis garb, too. Better than your average Friday night turnout at the Legion.

And now this S&M performing dog!

The crazy mutt deserves the ten-dollar cocktail Judy has just bought him. Usually she finds the rubber fetish scene a tad repulsive, but tonight is the night of any nights to make allowances. Everyone deserves a good time on Halloween.

She pushes her way to the front of the crowd, where Rover sits expectantly at the heels of his mistress.

"Here you are, then. Does he need a straw?"

"No, dear," smiles the Dominatrix, "but we'll have to undo his mask."

Judy pretends she knew this as she helps wrestle with straps and lacings on the rubber-bound slave, all the time clutching the drink in her armpit. Eventually, the hood comes off.

"Jesus, Mary, and Joseph!"

Judy lets the piña colada fall – *ka-chunk*! – on the carpet.

"Holy cow, it's Jack!"

Indeed it is. Looking up at her, a loose strand of hair sticking to his sweaty cheek, is her ex-husband. In all his pathetic glory. Who'd have guessed?

Shocked, Judy follows the drink to the floor. She is possessed by a fit of screaming, howling laughter.

"What's going on over there?" asks Murray. "Sounds like a circus."

Alex swallows. The tingling in his teeth is making everything into one large whorl. He hopes he isn't going to puke.

"It's Cherry Beach," he mumbles, recognizing the tall, lanky SS guard. "I bet she's doing her Ilse, Queen of the . . ."

His voice trails off as he spots the cause of all the ruckus.

"Holy Macarooni!"

Curled up on the floor, clutching her sequined stomach as if to stop the gales of hysteria pouring out of her, is Elvis Presley. But not just any old Elvis.

Alex feels himself turn blue. Somehow he ends up leaning against a wall, a concerned Murray fussing at his elbow.

"What is it? Are you OK, mate?"

"It's my Mom."

"What?"

"My Mom. Elvis is my Mom. And that," Alex chances another glance at the sweating slave in rubber who is trying to hide behind Cherry Beach's ankles.

"That's my Dad."

Downstairs, toward the edge of the main dance floor, Liberty Hanna lies draped over an ornate catafalque. She moans and foams blood at the mouth for the (so-far) titillation of passersby. If she could open her jaw wider, she would scream, except that everything along her right side is numb and she's having problems breathing, let alone shouting.

That's the last time she wears pink for Halloween.

She suspects she may have broken something in her neck, but it's hard to tell, what with all the drugs racing through her system. It was certainly a spectacular fall to the sepulchre from the balcony above. All legs and arms and flashing strobe lights.

No one had seen her.

"Oh look, a zombie!" shrieks a passing boogey-woogey-man. "Hey there, Zombie! Happy Halloween!"

Liberty tries to mouth "help" or "call an ambulance," but the burble from her lips sounds more like "you're welcome." Damn. She fits right in with the decor.

A tingling rises up her leg. Disco lights pulse through her eyelashes. Dry ice kisses her fingers. Her ego melts. Unconsciousness can't be far away.

sugarpop
zombies

(A Christmas Cautionary Tale)

P ink. A zillion pink bubbles in every direction. Wide-eyed unicorns cavort with flower-bedecked hippopotamuses in a rainbow-glutted butterfly sunset. Everything is sugarspun twinkles with candy-pastel ponies and starfish.

Liberty Hanna grunts, rolls over, and recalls that she's in hospital. Her personal TV plays Christmas ads for little girls' toys.

And that weird young woman is sitting in the visitor's chair by the bed. She's a serious-looking, ponytailed girl in a battered, green leather jacket. Just the sight of her makes Liberty feel queasy.

"Hi, Lib. You're awake, I see."

"What . . . who are you again?"

"I'm Rose. D'you recognize me yet?"

"Nope."

Six days in hospital and Liberty's still suffering from amnesia. Oh, she can remember the tedious details: her name, her address, five different social insurance numbers, her shoe size, and that she ovulates on the full moon.

But the rest of it's blank. She's had to rely on others to explain how she's ended up in hospital. Something must have happened to give her two broken ribs, a snapped collar bone, a green-stick fracture in her fibula and an extensive concussion. (The missing finger on her right hand is, apparently, an ancient injury.)

From what she can gather from the nurses, there'd been an accident at a Halloween party: she'd taken too many drugs and thrown herself off the balcony.

Drugs? It couldn't be. Someone must have spiked the punch.

Besides, her outfit (now in a plastic bag beneath her bed) is much too normal to be a Halloween costume. A pink and mauve ensemble that would go down just as well in the office as it would at a smart dinner party.

She's a little confused about the honey-kissed wig, but since her own hair is so short and ugly, it doesn't surprise her. Perhaps she'd had to hack off a bad perm.

"Remind me again how I'm supposed to know you."

"We live together."

"You're my roommate?"

Rose pulls a face. "How many times do I have to tell you?" She rises from her chair, hands on hips. "You're my girlfriend, you stupid dyke!"

Liberty's left eyelid twitches as this concept pushes its way through her synapses.

No! She pulls the hospital sheets over her head, shutting out the evil words, hoping for the sweet smell of liniment to envelop her. She tries to imagine herself back in the land of girlie-girl daisy-kissed bubblegum.

Lesbian! Scrambled candyfloss!

"Trick or treat!"

Halloween may be over for another year, but not for eight-year-old Brock Bloor. He's working the neighbourhood for the sixth afternoon in a row.

On Halloween proper, his crack-addict uncle had confiscated all his booty, with the excuse that sugar is bad for the metabolism. Which, as far as Brock is concerned, is a load of pooh. Sugar is brilliant. Sugar is fantastic. Sugar is a better rush than that Ritalin crap any day.

"Isn't Halloween over, young man?"

"I'm a diabetic orphan and my Evil Uncle keeps stealing my insulin!" chirps Brock. "If you're out of candy, I accept chocolate."

In this fashion, over the past six days, he's managed to stuff three pillowcases with jawbreakers, fizzballs and toffee chews. He has enough to keep him buzzing clear through to New Year's.

Inside the front gate to his uncle's house, Brock checks that the coast is clear. He then clambers up the fence, onto the raccoon-proof composter and up to the first crook in the horse chestnut tree. From there, he inches his way up to his branch, where he has the other two of his Auntie's floral pillowcases hidden amongst the turning leaves – tied to the cord of his dressing-gown and hitched off to a branch for safety.

"Shoo!"

Brock frightens away a nosy squirrel before nestling himself against his branch and setting to the task of choosing which candy to eat now, which candy to hoard in the tree.

Ten minutes later, there are little blue stars bursting at the edge of his vision. And he's giggling uncontrollably, his hands all sticky with sugar.

"Brock! What are you doing up there! I'm telling Mom!"

Damn. It's soppy cousin Martin.

The best defense is offense. Reaching out, Brock snaps off a sprig of horse chestnuts in their spiky casings.

"Bombs away! Ka-pow! Ka-pow! Die, Martin you gay drip!"

▼

Holy lesbian army! The bed is surrounded.

Liberty gulps, pulls the covers back over her head, counts to twelve, then resurfaces. They're still there. Half a dozen misfits of nature – with that Rose in the middle of 'em all.

They're all smiling lesbian smiles at her in a most disconcerting manner.

"She doesn't look too bad," says one.

"Hey, you could drop her off the CN Tower and she'd just break her ankle," says another.

"What's with the wig?"

Liberty screams inwardly. Aloud, she demands to know what's going on, who everyone is and what the jiminy heck did they think they were doing making goo-goo eyes at her.

"Did she just say 'jiminy heck'?"

"Shh!" says Rose. "She's suffering from amnesia. She doesn't recognize any of us."

"Bet she remembers this," says one purple-haired girl, lifting up her T-shirt to reveal a set of pierced nipples.

Liberty recoils. Gak! They're all monsters!

Grinning like a cornered chimpanzee, she hits the Nurse

Alert Button. Not just once, but over and over.

Help! SOS! *Mayday!* *Mayday!*

But the nurse doesn't come to her rescue, and the clutch of lesbians is insistent. They display their tattoos, they recount old stories, they even try to kiss her – all in an effort to jog her memory.

Liberty immerses herself in the land of TV Xmas toy commercials in an effort to tune them out. "Each set sold separately," she murmurs. "Batteries not included."

"I'll replace your batteries, you old whore," barks Rose, snapping off the TV.

Silence.

"Look," retorts Liberty, unable to take it any longer. "If ever I was a lesbian, I don't think I am anymore, OK? So you can all just go away."

Rose glares and sucks her lip.

"Methinks you need another bonk on the head."

Two weeks in the hospital and Liberty Hanna is pronounced fit enough to be released to the outside world. Rose is aghast. Physically, Liberty's on the mend. She can hobble around without crutches and no longer needs the dressing on her ribs.

Mentally, however, it's another story. This New Liberty still has severe amnesia, has developed a penchant for the pink, frilly and pasteloid, and worse, is a total homophobe. She'll withdraw into a television-ogling coma at the mere mention of Lesbos. The hospital couldn't see anything wrong with this, and besides, they needed the bed.

"Welcome home!"

Rose ushers Liberty into the warehouse studio.

"Holy cow, what a dump! Do I really live here?" Liberty adjusts the blond wig on her head and squints about. "It looks like an abattoir."

Rose, doing her best to maintain a Russ Meyer cool, helps Liberty over to the couch, which has been set up for her arrival.

"Jog any memory cells yet?"

"This is a joke, right?"

"Yeah, just like that lesbian thing."

Liberty gives Rose a pained smile and clicks on the TV.

"Right then," decides Rose after ten minutes have gone by. "Have a look at this."

She hauls out a large photo album – it must be six inches thick – and, after pausing for a couple seconds as if making up her mind, she lugs it over to the couch. She stands towering over her one-time girlfriend.

"I was gonna lead you through the last five years of your life," she says, weighing the album in her hands. "But this may be just as effective."

Whack!

Liberty tastes something warm and salty in the back of her nose. The TV splits into a double image for a moment before returning to normal. Then: pain.

"Ow!" she yelps. "What was that for?"

"Put it this way," says Rose. "If I were you, I'd hope you'd do the same for me."

Whack!

▼

The coast is clear.

Brock sneaks out of his room, down the stairs and along the landing to his Uncle Bob's bedroom. Revenge courses through his young veins. They'll be sorry!

Eight years old is a tad early to be harbouring such thoughts, but Brock Bloor has had a head start on most. By the time he was five, it had been drummed into him that he was an "unwanted child." At six, he learned that he owed his existence to a leaky condom.

It took him a while to learn what that meant. But he sure as hell knows now.

He's been around a bit, has young Brock. From drag queens to crack dens, he's seen it all. Most recently, Social Services stepped in and forced him back to his worst nightmare: sharing a room with his cousin Martin (the gay drip!) at his Auntie Marg and Uncles Bob 'n Al's house. Otherwise known as the zoo.

It's a horror show. Martin is a soppy dishcloth. Auntie Marg is two yards of yellowing teeth. Uncle Bob is a crack addict and Uncle Al is nothing but a big girl's lumberjack shirt. More ghastly guardians would be difficult to imagine.

Right now they've supposedly confined him to the prison of his lower bunk bed after a major war earlier on.

"You sneaky little bastard," Uncle Al had called him. "Where did you get all this?"

Punished for having Halloween candy. His swag confiscated, the only souvenir allowed was a huge pumpkin button the size of Auntie Marg's mouth. There was nothing for it but to throw a tantrum.

"No more Ritalin for you, young man!"

Ha! Adults are so dumb!

Uncle Bob's room smells of aftershave and mildewed socks. Brock makes a beeline for the bedside cabinet, the place where all the secrets are kept, and the last known hiding place of the Ritalin.

He finds a few porn mags, a bottle of something stinky, and some tubes of something gooey. Twenty bucks, which he pockets. No Ritalin. Uncle Bob must have sold it again.

But no matter: Brock's deficient attentions are transfixed by the box of Trojans. Opening them up, a small plastic baggie falls out. Uncle Bob's secret sugar stash!

Only it tastes nasty. Bitter. And it makes his mouth go numb. What a cheat! He dumps the rest of it on the carpet.

Grasping his Halloween button in his fist, Brock bends back the clasp. "Here's one more little prick in the world," he announces, lancing a condom pack with the pin. "And another. And another."

His eyes bulging and his teeth gritted, he goes through every condom in the box.

"Give me a set of the sultry zebra, three-quarter inch, please."

"Excellent choice."

Liberty sighs and settles herself at the friendly manicurist's table; she proffers her right hand for treatment. Camouflage. The missing middle digit reminds her of an unknown past. It's a past with which she would rather not have any connection, despite Rose's attempts to jolt her back into it.

To wit: she has two new bruises on her head and one on her shoulder where Rose dropped a heavy ashtray on her.

Well, thank God she'd snuck out of there before she'd gotten herself killed by that maniac. From now on, life is going to be pinky and perky. Sweetness and femininity. None of that lesbian garbage.

A gaggle of children goes by the salon window. They're all wrapped up in fluffy lilacs and salmons and Easter-egg yellows. Each child totes a happy Santa balloon from the parade. How cute, thinks Liberty, as her maternal instincts kick in. Wouldn't it be simply adorable to get married and have kiddies of her own?

"Er . . . excuse me?"

"What is it?"

The manicurist nods at Liberty's fingerstub.

"I can give you a 10 percent discount, if you'd like."

Liberty smiles and thanks her. The past has some advantages, after all.

The Pearson Centre Mall is sagging halfway through its Christmas marathon. The stamina required to get through to the January sales is, as always, Herculean. Few are up to the challenge. Most will succumb to exhaustion, nausea, and overexposure before the holidays really start.

This morning the crowds are sparse. The sales staff, hired especially for the season, easily outnumber the shoppers. But it's early in the day. Things will, undoubtedly, pick up come the lunch hour.

The ubiquitous decorations are getting dusty – some of them have, after all, been in place since before Halloween. A spangly disease has spread throughout the mall. From haemorrhoidal crusted pine-cone pyramids to flaked and scrobiculate snowmen, nothing escapes the holiday blight.

Liberty Hanna waltzes through the food court with a smile on her lips and a spring to her step. Anyone who knew her less than a month ago could be forgiven for thinking this is someone else entirely. Gone are the black leathers, the army boots, the body piercings. Instead, Liberty sports a blonde back-combed wig, fuchsia pumps, and enough frills and flounces to smother an Italian wedding cake.

Apart from this obvious personality change (along with a vehement rejection of her lesbian past), she seems to be coping with her amnesia fairly well. It's surprising how little memory one actually needs to cope with modern life.

". . . and a partri-idge in a pear tree!"

Liberty sings gaily along with the Muzak, deftly sidestepping a throng of teenagers outside an electronics store. She has much to be happy about.

She's escaped from that nightmare of a warehouse where Rose, the psychotic lesbian, kept trying to bash her over the head in an effort to change her sexuality. Now she's staying at the Y.

And she has a job she adores! With children! Hurrah!

With her eyeballs popping like an aerobics instructor on an adrenaline high (or, perhaps, a goldfish starved of oxygen), Liberty flounces through a door next to the underground parking lot marked *Employees Only*.

Whoever thought that going to work could be so much fun?

▼

"I'll kill you, you evil little gargoyle!"

Brock darts behind the sofa to escape his Uncle Bob and runs smack into soppy Martin. Damn. So near, yet so far.

"Got him, Dad!"

Uncle Bob catches up, twists one of Brock's eight-year-old arms behind his back and pushes his ugly mustache into Brock's face.

"What did you do with my fucking coke, you pipsqueak bastard?"

"Coke?"

It takes Uncle Bob a few spluttering minutes to explain that he's talking about the white powder that Brock had plundered from the bedside cabinet.

"Oh, yuck," says Brock. "I thought it was fizz candy."

"Jesus!" Uncle Bob's neck glows red. "There was half a gram left in there!"

"It tasted vile, you could have poisoned me."

Uncle Bob gives Brock such a backhander, it sends him

spinning over the sofa and into the dining-room table.

"Just what do you think you're doing, Robert Bloor!"

It's Auntie Marg. She's standing in the doorway to the kitchen, her expression all frozen toothy smiles of concern and goodness.

"I said, 'what do you think you're doing?'!"

"The little bast . . ."

"No hitting Brock!" steams Auntie Marg. "Think what the Social Services would say!"

"Uncle Bob's just angry that I threw out his cocaine," mutters Brock, massaging his head where it hit the table.

"Cocaine?"

Auntie Marg's head snaps back like a synchronized swimmer's. Her toothy smile reasserts itself with doubled intensity. Swiftly she drags Uncle Bob into the kitchen and slams the door. Brock listens to the muffled shouts with a sneaky grin on his face. He sticks out his tongue at Martin.

Eventually Auntie Marg emerges with the First Aid Kit.

"How's my brave little soldier doing?" she coos, as she dabs witch hazel onto Brock's bruises. "Maybe we can think of something nice to do this afternoon."

"Can we kill Martin?"

"Hmm." Auntie Marg ponders an alternative. "How would you like to go visit Santa?"

"At the Pearson Centre Mall?"

She glances at her watch. "Er . . . sure, if you like."

Brock plays his cards as gently as he dare.

"Can we visit the World of Candy?"

"Well, I don't know about . . ."

"*Please* can we visit the World of Candy, can we, please, please, *please!*"

Santa's Grotto at the Pearson Centre Mall is in the epicentre of Toytown, a maze of product so cleverly placed that no matter what your budget, you're bound to pass something to suit.

At the entrance to the Grotto proper, right beneath two giant crisscrossed candy canes, you're greeted by the Sugar Plum Fairy.

Liberty Hanna.

In a glistening silver tutu, matching tiara and ballet slippers, she's supposed to be *en pointe* whenever anyone's watching. The best Liberty can manage, however, is one foot at a time. But this she executes with enough fairy *élan* to please her employer, Cecil, the souvenir photogift elf.

"Welcome to Santa's Grotto!" she chants, waving her battery-powered magic wand that blinks on and off with a disconcerting buzz. "Welcome!"

As each child comes forward, it is the Sugar Plum Fairy's job to determine (a) how old the child is, (b) what gender the child is, and (c) whether they would like to have their picture taken with Santa for fifteen dollars a pop.

She then relays this information to Cecil, who takes the money from the anxious parents.

The best part of the job comes when she admits each child to the magical land of Santa's Grotto by gesticulating wildly with her wand while surreptitiously opening the gate. She can almost see a gazillion cartoon stars envelop each child as she works her enchantment. Once, in her enthusiasm, she accidentally clipped a small girl in the ear, for which she'd felt so guilty that she gave the child a free trip to Santa.

"Welcome to Santa's Grotto!" she chants. "Each item sold separately!"

"What are we doing at the Pearson Fucking Centre Mall in the middle of the Christmas rush, Phoebe?"

Phoebe stops. Glares.

"Do you wanna find your girlfriend or not?"

Rose bites her lip and obediently follows Phoebe through the crowd. If Liberty can be found amongst this Yuletide rabble, it could be worth suffering the thousand and one indignities and perfumes.

The past month has been a nightmare. The hospital hadn't been too hard to deal with. The amnesia had a spark of originality to it. It was Liberty turning into a bona fide Stepford Wife that had been too much to bear. But even giving her a few whacks on the head hadn't knocked the flounces out of her.

Then two weeks ago, she vanished.

Poor Rose went so far as to put up "Lost Girlfriend" notices on hydro poles downtown. Other than half a dozen crank calls of the obvious nature, the exercise proved fruitless. That is until yesterday, when Phoebe Spadina called to say that Liberty had been sighted. At the Pearson Centre Mall, apparently.

"There, see!" whispers Phoebe, pointing excitedly through a stack of Dreamdouche Fergie dolls in the toy department. "Recognize her?"

Rose squints. She's looking at Santa's Grotto.

"Welcome children!" rasps the Sugar Plum Fairy at the entrance gate. "Each set sold separately!"

"Omigod," gulps Rose, recognizing the voice. "It's her!"

▼

Under the supervision of his Auntie Marg, Brock Bloor is as excited as any other eight-year-old to be visiting the Pearson Centre Mall. He's had a few disappointments with Santa in the past, so he's not raising his hopes on that score, but the World of Candy holds a promise that can always be relied upon.

Auntie Marg, however, knows what sugar does to Brock's metabolism, and is determined not to let her charge get within a hundred yards of the place.

Slowly and inevitably, Brock is dragged towards the hated Santa's Grotto up at the far end of the mall. Time is running out. Checking the stolen cash in his pocket (swiped from his Uncle Bob's bedside cabinet), he decides to put Plan E into action.

"I gotta go to the washroom," he whines, squirming uncomfortably.

"Didn't you go before we came?"

"Yeah, but I gotta go again."

Auntie Marg girds herself with a toothed smile of exasperation, then relents.

"All right, but be quick about it."

The very second he enters the washroom, Brock doubles

back on his tracks. He peeks around the tiled corner. Auntie Marg is searching for a place to sit and wait – it's too early in the game for her suspicions to be raised. Quickly, he nips into the food court and ducks behind a trash bin.

Freedom!

"I can't believe it," whispers Rose. "I mean, look at all those sequins! Who does she think she's kidding?"

"What are you going to do?" asks Phoebe. "Should we kidnap her from Santa?"

"Hmm."

Rose considers her options. She could try giving Liberty another bonk on the head, but seeing how previous attempts had failed so miserably, she doesn't put much store in that remedy. She could attempt a conversation with this girlie-girl zombie. Then again, she could, as Phoebe suggests, try her hand at a little Sugar Plum Fairy abduction.

Or she could toss in her cards and go home. Find herself another girl for the winter.

She sighs, then turns to Phoebe.

"Fancy a drink, somewhere?"

Purple Grape Fizzbangs! Tangerine Zingfrutti Gummies! Sour Lime Crunchnerds! Supabanana Taffy Chews!

Brock staggers out of the World of Candy, his pockets bulging, his eyes reeling, his heart pumping. He's snarfled his way through at least ten dollars' worth of sugar. The resultant charge rushing through his system makes him zip about like a digital piranha.

At the fountain he digs into his pocket to find a penny, but can only find a handful of Sherbet Twists. In his intoxicated state he decides they'll do and tosses them in.

"I wish for three more wishes!"

He balances his way around the edge of the fountain, clambering over the backs of tired shoppers and disinterested teenagers.

"I wish for twelve more wish . . ."

"Brock Bloor!"

Uh-oh. It's Auntie Marg, over by the escalators. There's only one thing for it: escape to the last place she'd think of looking.

Focusing loosely on the end of the mall, Brock makes a run for it.

▼

"Welcome to Santa's Grotto. Would you like your picture taken with Santa for fifteen dollars?"

"Um . . ." The little boy who'd come running up so eagerly a few moments ago looks uncomfortable. "Um . . . I don't have any money left."

"Well, where's your mummy?" sings Liberty, "Perhaps mummy can help you."

"I'm an orphan." He glances around him in a panic. "How much just to get in – quick?" he huffs.

"Five dollars," smiles Liberty.

"All I got is this," says the kid, offering up a bulging paper bag of sweets. "It's worth at least ten bucks. Will it get me in?"

"Well, I don't know."

"Pl-eeeez," he whines. "Pretty fairy lady, *please* let me in, it's a matter of life or death!"

Liberty's heart melts. He called her pretty!

"Well, perhaps just one."

She picks out a paper-twist, the size of a small onion. "What flavour's this?"

"That's a Dynamite Tropicana Fizzbomb, silly," chirps the kid. "Better hold onto your hat!"

Feeling most maternal, Liberty waves him into the Grotto with her magic wand. She chuckles at the cuteness of childhood, untwists her Fizzbomb and pops the confection into her mouth.

Mmmm. It's quite tasty. Strawberry. Lime. Pineapple. An unknown flavour: sharp and acidic. Then a sudden explosion in the back of her mouth, bubbling up into her sinuses.

Fzzh-crack-phh!

What's this? Liberty's synapses react to the chemical intrusion. An electric memory of black leather jackets and punk music floods back. Something shifts deep within her cortex. The teeter-totter of memory adjusts itself; her snoozing ego stretches, yawns, and bursts through her id to the surface.

She's back.

"Scrambled fucking tofu!" she screams, staring in disbelief at her Sugar Plum Fairy outfit. "Boy, was that ever one giant K-hole!"

happy wacky new year monkey

(A Fin-de-Siècle Melodrama)

Early

The sky is a stunning blue. The grass a surreal green. In the distance there are rolling hills, bubbling brooks, butterflies, puffy clouds and daisies. A Perfect Spring Day.

Foxley Dovercourt shakes his hair loose as if surfacing after a dive. He gulps oxygen, leans against a tree; beads of sweat pepper the back of his neck. He loosens his collar and takes a swig of mineral water. He then dabs his brow with a towel that seems to have appeared out of nowhere – as does the voice that comes with it.

"Are you OK, buddy?"

"Sure. Fine."

"Hang on in there, huh? One more run-through should do it."

"I believe you. Thousands wouldn't."

Foxley takes a deep breath, grits his teeth, and prepares to plunge back into claustrophobia – back into the nylon sweatbox.

Back into the rabbit's head.

Many are the ways Foxley Dovercourt would prefer to be spending his New Year's Eve: dancing, drinking, laughing, weeping, falling down stairs, etc. Dressing up as the Easter Bunny, getting chased by some chimpanzee over Astroturf under blazing hot lights for fourteen hours for some discount furniture warehouse commercial isn't on his list of ways to ring in the new.

But then, it's always frightful what an actor will do for a thousand bucks (give or take the odd 15 percent for meal penalties or an agent).

Oh, to be back home, thinks Foxley. Home in his snug apartment, preparing for this auspicious evening in an elegant, preferably drunken, frame of mind.

Reality check.

His apartment isn't snug. It's minuscule – an elevator would be more capacious. Worse, there's a Brussels-sauerkraut-burnt-turkey odour leaking through the heating vents ever since Xmas, the neighbours watch WWF TV at full blast, and if he doesn't get to the liquor store in half an hour, it's Crown Royal for auld lang syne tonight.

"You're Fox Dovercourt, right?"

Fox smirks, nods.

"Your sister called Production this morning."

"I heard."

No kidding, he's heard. The makeup girl told him, both wardrobe and continuity told him, three PAs and an irate CRAFT boy told him. He's surprised it hasn't been announced over the hockey game that everyone's listening to on their headphones. Hey, everyone! An actor got a personal call while on set! Remember the name: Foxley Dovercourt. Blacklisted for life, along with anyone who looks like him.

He could just kill Pandora, if he ever gets his paws on her. Lucky for her she's on the West Coast.

Not that distance seems to be a deterrent; the past three days she's been calling non-stop. Foxley's voice mail is filled to the brim with his younger sister bemoaning, beweeping, and becursing her most recent breakup. Ex-boyfriend this, ex-boyfriend that. Sob, sob, sob. She must be on some kind of long-distance plan.

"Ready to go when you are, buddy. Last take of the day. We'll get it this time, for sure."

Foxley struggles with the Easter Bunny noggin for a while, then sighs.

"I've got a problem," he says, squinting under the lights. "My glasses are stuck in this fucking rabbit's head."

A new year, a new city!

Stanley Park gazes through the bus window at the unfamiliar city lights. He tries to ignore the sensation of lightheadedness as he glides into the bus terminus with mere hours left on the clock before the new year. He feels like a kid again.

It's taken three days to get here from the West Coast. Seventy-one hours, sixteen minutes through the mountains, across the prairies, the prairies, the prairies, the prairies, then over the lakes and down. He could really use a shower and a horizontal bed. He's sick of sleeping in the bus seat, his head shaking against the window, his legs just kinda squished up any old how.

A decent meal would be nice, too. He's been on a diet of fried chicken, burgers, and pop: the best the highway stops could offer.

He stares at the grey neon-lit city through the window. Despite the sad reflections of an exhaust-ridden utilitarian architecture, he decides the trip has been worth it. He's free.

Free from Pandora.

Screw Pandora and her thinly veiled pretensions of monogamy. Or rather: don't screw Pandora. For the past year Stanley's been discovering a whole new world: boys. And now here he is in the Mecca of Boystown!

"Everybody out!"

Everyone files outside to reclaim their baggage. Stan breathes his first lungfuls of city air. The Big Smoke!

Practical details crowd his brain. He has nowhere to go. No one to call. He has five hundred dollars and a skateboard. In his pocket he has an ad for a downtown steam bath, where he intends to stay for the first few nights. He must be crazy, but does he care? Not he!

He points out his backpack in the cargo bin. The driver hauls it out for him.

"Holy stinking pulp mills, buddy! What you got in there?" A foul stench hits the back of Stan's throat. "Smells like rotten fish."

It is, indeed, a rotten fish. The remains of a BC sockeye salmon, to be precise. It's shoved down the side of his knapsack and wrapped in the lyrics of a song Pandora once wrote for him: "Twisted Love."

For three long days and nights this bundle of joy has been travelling in the warm bowels of the bus. A vile liquid now seeps throughout Stan's worldly belongings, and has probably ruined his stash of skunk weed.

He should have known Pandora wouldn't let him go without some kind of parting shot.

Künstlicher Schweinehund!

In the bus station washrooms, Stan upends his bag; dumps everything out onto the tiled floor. He endures the snickers of the entire male population of the bus as they relieve themselves. Soon, however, he is alone and can assess the damage undisturbed.

A couple of T-shirts are ruined. Deepak Chopra, William Burroughs and Nostradamus are all beyond salvation – steeped in fish brine – which has to be an omen of some depth. His pot may or may not be OK, it's difficult to tell without smoking it. Everything reeks.

The hairs on the back of his neck prickle. He's being watched. He spins around.

Sitting in one of the cubicles, with the door ajar, is a sleek young man in a dark blue turtleneck. Smiling.

"Hey there, brother," comes a soft, acrylic voice. "Need a hand?"

Stan flushes to his roots. Immediate excitement swells within. "Um . . . What did you have in mind?"

"You just get off the bus?"

Shoving his stuff back into his pack, Stan shrugs. "New year, new city."

"Come over here then. I'll get you started."

Three minutes later, the two of them are wanking in the cubicle, pants around their ankles. "Oh yeah, my stinky brother," moans the nylon lad, toiling away. "I could play all night with you. Where are you staying?"

"Um . . . actually," says Stan, "I was thinking of staying the first few nights at The Gentleman's Quarters."

There is a short pause while the mood shifts.

"You're a Lost Lamb."

The mood restores, but all eroticism has fled.

"You can't stay there!" beams the young man, hoisting himself back into his Stayprest trousers. "You must stay with us. Come."

Buttoning his own fly, Stan follows meekly. He is amazed at how easily he has allowed himself to be picked up. It isn't until he's sitting in the ecru plastic interior of a Ford station wagon (with wood side panelling) that he realizes the promise of more static-cling sex with the unnamed "us" has his heart a-pounding.

His new companion pauses with the keys in the ignition. "What's your name, O Stinky One?"

"Stan. Stanley. You?"

"Call me Brother Clarence."

And with that they roar off into the night, the muffler coughing and spluttering behind them.

Up, up, up in the air, cruising above a carpet of cloud that glows a gentle viridian in the dusk, Pandora Begbie weeps into her complimentary Chicken Kiev.

She's going through the tissues and antihistamines like there's no 1999. Her eyes are black as a panda's where her Earthwatch mascara has blotched. Weeping at high altitudes plays havoc on the sinuses and creates a vicious circle of pain.

It's all so hopeless.

She hasn't been able to get hold of her brother, she has no idea where she's going to find Stan, and she's just spent her last four hundred dollars on a plane ticket. She must be loopy.

What had possessed her to stuff that dead fish in his bag? Now he'll hate her for eternity, unless she can somehow persuade him to return to her ever-lovin' arms. And that simply has to be done in person. It shows commitment.

For in her soul of souls, Pandora is surely welded to Stanley, regardless of his dalliances in the university washrooms. He's not gay. Bisexual, perhaps, but not homosexual. Surely.

The I-Ching had confirmed it on her 364th consultation.

Thus here she is. New Year's Eve. On an airplane.

"Ladies and gentlemen, we're beginning our descent. Please return your seat and tray to the upright position."

Pandora prepares herself for the torture of landing.

The plane descends. Her ears ache. Her eyes tear. Her sinuses throb. She can't think. She puts her watch back four hours.

▼

"Please be open! Please be open!"

Foxley Dovercourt mutters his mantra to the liquor store gods as he phut-phuts through the streets on his moped.

Breathing is difficult in the Easter Bunny brainbox, but it was either that or blurred vision – and the New Year's Eve traffic is beginning to snarl. Until he gets home and finds his spare pair of Emergency Welfare Goggles, he's stuck with the darn thing.

His glasses are jammed irretrievably inside. No amount of cajoling, pulling with pliers, twisting or yanking, could persuade the spectacles to come loose from the infernal head. The Props

Department had run off to some party. There was nothing for him to do but parade through the streets like some freak.

At least the chimpanzee riding on his handlebars pulls focus from him. Somewhat.

Yup, chimp. The same party that had drawn the Props Department into its vortex had yanked the entire studio. For twenty seconds at the end of the shooting day there had been some balloons, streamers, and horns. Then everybody vanished. Leaving Foxley with his co-star, Jessica.

There she was, sitting in her canvas chair, sucking back a soda water, looking ultracasual in her diapers and Happy New Year tiara. She'd fixed him with a long, winsome stare before slowly getting up, lolloping over to him, and taking his hand.

As far as Foxley's concerned, the whole night so far is perfect. If, to give 1998 a swift boot up the arse, it takes riding through the streets in a rabbit's head and a chimpanzee on the handlebars, then that's what it takes.

He turns the corner. Blessed Residuals! The liquor store is still open!

At a brisk trot, Foxley enters, his monstrous head still on and Jessica riding his hip, her arms draped around his neck. The place is packed.

He runs down the aisles, searching for the Scotch section, blatantly ignoring the shrieks of astonishment.

"Hold it right there!"

After a moment, Foxley obeys. He is, after all, staring down the barrel of a gun. At the trigger end is a frightened security guard.

"OK mister, nice and slow. Just don't hurt the monkey."

"Welcome to our meeting house, Stan. Please remove your shoes."

Stan looks uncomfortably about him. They are in some kind of a vestibule. Everything is very clean. The walls are of a glowing pine, accented with blue. Stan adds his green Reeboks to the lineup of running shoes on the mat. His erection has vanished.

"Where are we?" He eyes the Art Deco crucifix-cum-flower vase suspiciously. "I thought we were going to your place?"

"This is our place, Stanley," says Brother Clarence in his soft monotone. "We are the Church of Jesus Christ and the Latent Gay Saints. Welcome."

Yikes!

"Er . . . I don't think this is gonna work out," gulps Stan. "I just need somewhere to grab a shower. Me 'n Jesus don't mix."

"Oh no, Stanley." Brother Clarence grips Stan's elbow and whispers lecherously in his ear. "Jesus goes down well with everyone. Especially we sinners." As if to illustrate his point, he flings open the main doors to reveal a dozen men all dressed in dark, unnatural fibres. They sit on hard, wooden chairs in a circle, each bobbed head turning to face the newcomers.

"Greetings, my gay brethren," intones Brother Clarence. "I bring with me a new Lost Lamb from the Toilets of Purgatory."

He gestures grandly at Stan.

"Say hello to Brother Stanley."

Dusk

"Paging Foxley Dovercourt. Will Foxley Dovercourt please contact the Information Desk on the Arrivals Level."

Pandora Begbie winces as her brother's professional stage name is broadcast over the public address system. There'd been no response to a page for Grant Begbie, so she'd tried Foxley Dovercourt instead. It dawns on her that he might not have come to pick her up at all. Poor Pandora. In her state, this could be the last straw.

She's beyond tears. Having wept throughout her budget flight from Lotus Land, her sinuses are flushed raw and her ears refuse to pop. Emotionally sluiced, she craves antidepressants. Her only glimmer of hope is that she might get a good song out of the whole experience.

At the luggage carousel she claims her bags. Her guitar, her carryalls. Since she didn't know how long it would take to find her soon-to-be-ex-ex-boyfriend in a strange city, she'd packed as much as she could carry – and then a few bags more. There are three lockers of her stuff still at the airport on the West Coast, should she ever return.

She's indulging a fantasy: she'll arrive in the Big City, find Stan (with her brother's help), apologize for the dead fish in his backpack, and profess her love as the clock strikes midnight on the old year. Then there will be a kiss – a big wet one – and everything will be hunky-dory.

Well, it's getting dark already. She seems to have miscalculated the time difference. Her dream is already wilting under the weight of reality.

"Greetings, Brother Stanley!" They all speak as one.

Gott in Himmel! Stanley Park shakes his head in horror. The last thing he'd expected when the polyester stranger picked him up in the bus station washrooms was to be dragged into the midst of a group of religious fruitcakes. But here he is: fresh off the boat and about to be indoctrinated into the Church of Jesus Christ and the Latent Gay Saints. No, not indoctrinated. Fraternized. Raped.

"Er, I don't think this is going to work, guys," he announces.

"Don't deny it, Stanley," says Brother Clarence. "You know it's what you want. You belong with us."

Stan stares at them: a dozen identically dressed boys, svelte, Stayprest slacks, dark turtlenecks, pudding-basin cuts and glazed eyes. A couple of them sport wire-rimmed spectacles.

Then he compares himself: army pants, parka, Stüssy shirt, scraggy shoulder-length hair, skateboard. He stinks of fish and three days on the bus.

"Don't get offended," he says, as reasonably as he can, "but I'm really not into group scenes, you know?"

"We are all equal in the eyes of Our Gay Lord," says one, standing up.

"God is faithful," quotes another. "He will not suffer ye to be tempted above that ye are able."

At which point, they ceremoniously surround him. Brother Clarence reaches out and lovingly caresses Stan's cheek . . .

Stan's Kung Fu has never been good. In a flash, despite his best efforts, he's pinned to the floor. Flighty hands caress him, undress him.

Off comes his coat. His socks.

"Sweet Jesus, No!"

"Sweet Jesus, Yes!"

Poor Stanley! Though no stranger to group sex, this particular arrangement has lost all its appeal. Frankly, it hadn't had much to begin with.

"This one's a bit on the ripe side, Brother Clarence."

"Smells like fish."

"Smells like a woman."

They stop, caught for a moment in their misogyny. Stan feels the grip on him loosen. It's now or never, he thinks. He summons his strength.

With the force that comes with desperation, he makes a lunge for his backpack. He manages a firm hold on his skateboard.

Thwak! Thwak!

Using his trusty board as a bludgeoning shield, he extricates himself from the cultish Christians' clutches. He swipes Brother Clarence across the elbow. Another brother around the knees. In this manner, he clears a pathway to the door and then – H*eilige Schwule!* – he escapes out the door and into the street.

Barefoot, coatless, and somewhat dazed, he coasts down the sidewalk. It's bitterly cold, but he doesn't give a hoot. He doesn't dare turn to look behind him.

"Should old acquaintance be forgot . . . and I forget the words!" sings Foxley Dovercourt, bounding up the front steps to his building.

What a night! Almost arrested at the liquor store, he's lucky the security guard believed his tale of woe. They'd confiscated the chimpanzee, given him a warning, and after all is said and done, he's somehow managed to acquire a bottle of ten-year-old Scotch without paying for it.

"Dum-de dum-de dum-de dum, for the something auld lang syne!"

He stops.

There's an obstacle by the intercom to his building. Without his glasses, it's a blur of amorphous colour.

"Hi, Grant."

Fox scrabbles for his spectacles, then remembers they're currently stuck inside the giant rabbit's head he has tucked under his arm. He dons the head to get a clearer picture of what his worst suspicions already know to be the truth.

Sitting atop a ramshackle bundle of luggage – a guitar, a couple of hockey bags, carryalls, and overnight bags – is a girl with purple-and-green hair, an Afghan coat, and love beads.

Pandora.

"What the fuck are you doing here, Pandy?"

"Didn't you get my message?"

"In a word: no." His voice is muffled by the rabbit's head. "Actually, I stopped listening after the first six. Something about breaking up with your boyfriend, wasn't it?"

Pandora bursts into tears. "He turned gay on me, Grant," she wails. "Why do they always turn gay on me?!"

Foxley shrugs. Now there's a question he daren't answer.

"I've got to get him back," she continues. She flaps her arms hopelessly in the air, jangling her Khartoumian bells. "I made a horrible mistake. I did something . . . awful, can you understand?"

Foxley sighs and starts wrestling with her bags. He'd better get her inside before someone calls the cops.

"You'll help me find him, won't you, Grant? You'll help me?"

Foxley pretends not to hear.

Later

There are only a few remaining hours in the old year.

Since arriving in town, Stanley Park has had his world shaken by the ankles. He stinks to high heaven, he's been half-raped by a group of religious gay fruitcakes, lost his shoes, his socks, his coat, and his knapsack with all its contents, including the five hundred dollars with which he was going to start his new life in the big city.

Fortunately, he still has his skateboard. Ol' Curb Climber.

Oblivious to the rules of the road, he coasts the wrong way down a wide street, the wind nipping at his bare tootsies.

He glances up, hoping to get his bearings, but soon realizes there are no mountain guides. He's in a city whose secrets are hidden to him. He's two and a half thousand miles from his last known mailing address. He has nowhere to go, no one to call.

And it's freezing. He curses himself for having been such an impulsive *Dummkopf*.

But it had been his decision, right? He'd wanted this: an adventure. A new pond, fresh pastures, an escape from Pandora's hysteria over him sucking a few cocks in the university washrooms.

He hadn't told her about the nights at the steam baths.

"*Scheisse!*"

He pulls to a stop, back wheels squeaking against cold concrete. His feet are blue. It's way too chilly to continue. Besides, how's he going to pay for a bathhouse with no money?

He has no option: he's going to have to go back for his clothes and his cash.

Furious, he spins around and retraces his tracks. An angry abandon enters his skating. He jumps the curb and plows around pedestrians and traffic alike. The landmarks blur by.

At the next intersection he narrowly escapes being mown down by a police cruiser. It appears out of his blind spot, gunning right at him. Stan saves himself against a parked car.

"Fuck you, *Schweine!*" He gives the roof of the cruiser a flat-palmed whack as it passes.

Police reflexes being what they are, the car gets halfway down the block before bumping to a halt. Then, inevitably, it reverses to level with him. The officer in the passenger seat is already on the radio. ". . . requesting a wagon. 822B on a skateboard. College and Bathurst."

Foxley Dovercourt pours himself a healthy glass of purloined Scotch, as well he ought, after fourteen hours on set dressed as the Easter Bunny and his gruelling experience in the liquor store. He flicks on the TV and plonks his ass down in his giant beanbag.

He tosses an evil glance at his sister, who is fussing over her bags around his couch. What couch? He can barely see it any more, it's so overladen with her crap. Incredible. From the moment Pandora traipsed through his door, her bags have bloomed, he swears, to five times their original size. She's like a rampant rainforest. A burst of tears, a tissued snuffle, a rummage in a ruptured holdall for antihistamines.

"Happy New Year," Fox says bitterly, raising his glass.

"I beg your pardon?" Pandora wiggles her finger in her ear, then hits herself twice around the head. "My eardrums still won't pop. Sorry."

Louder: "I said, 'What Are You Doing Here?'"

Pandora stops shaking out her tasselled, belled, and mirrored frocks. "Don't be such a prick," she sniffs. She stands frozen for a while before snapping out of her reverie and continuing, "I've come to get Stan back."

"Gosh, I'm sorry. It looked for a moment as if you're moving in."

"Your karma is so fucked, Grant."

"Bullshit." Fox takes a gulp of Scotch. "And stop calling me Grant. My name's Foxley now. I'm reincarnated, if you will. Foxley Dovercourt. Actor. I'm with Black Hole Talent."

With a renewed sense of purpose he goes to the couch and starts removing her stuff, piling it against the wall. Her bags, her guitar, her rubble.

"What are you doing?"

"I'm looking for my glasses. And your shit's in the way."

"Can't it wait?" As ever, Pandora is petulant. "I've got to find Stan."

"Have you tried looking in the steam baths yet?" quips

Foxley. "How long has he been in town?"

Pandora studiously consults her watch. She asks a few questions about time differences and attempts some mental arithmetic.

"Fuck, fuck, fuck, oh shit!" She looks imploringly at Foxley. "I think his bus gets in in ten minutes."

"So?"

"So, Mr. Foxley Dovercourt, famous actor, I need a ride to the bus station, don't I?"

Interlude

Warm sun and delicious sea breezes. A mysterious woman in white lounges in a deckchair by a beach-side pool, partly shaded by the palm-leaf overhang of the bar. She sips a margarita and flips through a copy of *Atlantic Fish Fancier*, the only English language magazine she could find on the island.

Island?

This is the tropical South Sea island of Mummichog, thousands of miles from the mainland and especially thousands of miles from the harsh winters of Northern North America. Ribbons of unspoiled beaches, five-star hotels, obsequious locals, and quaint little horse-drawn carriage rides through the market.

A beautiful island.

The mysterious woman, known only as "Whatserface" by the locals, sighs and reminds herself once again of the wonders of life insurance.

Perhaps tomorrow she'll go for a swim.

End of interlude

Riding in the back of a paddy wagon is a time-honoured mode of transportation. You meet the most interesting people!

Stanley's fellow travellers in this particularly charming vomit-encrusted Black Maria include two squeegee kids, one handcuffed drunk, a very sweaty guy in a red nylon track suit, and a chimpanzee in diapers. Either that, or it's someone doing an excellent imitation of a chimpanzee in diapers.

"Yup, it's a monkey," says one of the kids. "Check it out."

It's true. And there's a Happy New Year tiara in silver letters.

"I wonder what his crime was," ponders Stan, massaging his feet.

"Didn't pay his parking ticket," growls the drunk.

The paddy wagon jerks to a stop. Voices. The rear doors open up and uniforms block the light.

"Last stop of the evening!" announces one.

"Everybody out!" commands another.

"You, you, and you!" snaps the third, pointing sharply at one of the kids, the guy in the track suit, and then at Stanley. "Door on your right! Shoes off and onto the table!"

10, 9, 8 . . . Countdown

The bus station always gets its fair share of weirdos. As Foxley arrives on his moped with his sister riding pillion, it gets two more. Pandora, weeping ethnic beads and West Coast hempery, has her acoustic guitar slung across her back. Foxley wears the Easter Bunny head.

Before they've even pulled to a halt, Pandora is off the back and bounding over to the information desk, leaving Foxley to doff the hated rabbit noggin and shake his hair loose under the fluorescents.

Damn Pandora, he thinks. The last thing he wants to be doing on New Year's Eve is chasing after her most recent casualty *d'amour*. But this one had "turned gay on her" (as she so quaintly phrased it) and perhaps because of this Foxley feels a slight twinge of guilt. He'd always lorded his sexuality over Pandora as an impassable gulf separating them. Tonight the impasse has brought them together.

Pandora returns, breathless.

"Shit!" she huffs. "His bus came in over two hours ago."

"Oh well, then," mutters Foxley. "I guess we're out of luck."

"But no one remembers seeing him leave." She chews her lip. "He got off the bus, but he didn't leave the depot."

"Oh, like the whole world knows this Stanley Park guy?"

Pandora impersonates the height of sarcastic boredom as only she can.

"I stuck a dead fish in his luggage, dumbo. Everyone remembers that." She glances around as if looking for something. "Hmm. I bet I know where the sneaky turdburgler is."

And with that niggardly comment, she is off again. Once he sees where she's headed, Foxley follows, running.

Into the Men's Washrooms.

▼

The three of them who'd been singled out are in a yellowing municipal room at the police station. The sweaty guy in the red track suit will not shut up.

"This is too fucking much can you believe this like what have I done what am I being fucking arrested for I haven't even been arrested this is too fucking much, man, I'm telling you I'm going to call my lawyer, man, Jesusfak!"

Stan and the squeegee kid exchange a knowing glance.

Two officers enter and track-suit man goes mum.

"Listen up!"

In smirking tones the boys in blue announce that since this is New Year's Eve, and since none of them wanted to be working in the first place, time and a half notwithstanding, then there is bound to be someone who has to take the fall.

It is further explained that one of them (no telling which, unfortunately) has the required Saint John's Ambulance certificate to conduct a cavity search. All three of the detained suspects have aroused sufficient suspicion to warrant such measures. It's already been logged at the main desk, there's nothing anyone can do.

One of the officers starts playing the mouth-trumpet version of "The Stripper" as the other dons a pair of rubber gloves. The evening's entertainment is underway. Track-suit man starts up again.

"Hey, Chatty Cathy, put a sock in it."

"Where are your shoes?" Stan is asked.

"I lost them at a Gay Mormon Cult Indoctrination, didn't I?"

"Cheeky fuck, aren't you?"

And so it goes. In ten minutes, they are harassed out of their clothes.

They stand there, awkward, naked, their hands covering their genitals. Officer A goes through their belongings. Officer B approaches Stan.

"Right, then. Hands on the table. Bend over."

Here it comes, thinks Stan, the killer death probe. He has to admit the idea of getting screwed on New Year's Eve had been on his mind earlier, but not quite like this.

He braces himself, takes a deep breath, prays to high heaven that he isn't getting an erection and allows his butt cheeks to be spread and examined for contraband.

"Well surprise, surprise! Lookie here what I found!"

It's Officer A, over at the table. He's holding up the red track suit pants with one disdainful hand and a little glass vial of brownish powder in the other.

"I . . . er . . . what's that? I've never seen that before in my life!" splutters its supposed owner.

The officers are both, clearly, ecstatic, but they hide it beneath a world-weary brusqueness. "It's off to the races with you, buddy boy," they grumble, handcuffing their new-found drug baron and whisking him, still naked and complaining, out of the room.

Silence. Stan looks at the kid. The kid looks back at him.

"Nice tattoo."

Fish. Rotting fish. In the waste bin. Bingo!

Pandora pulls out the stinking, soggy remnants of the hand-scrawled sheet music in which she'd wrapped the sockeye salmon. "Twisted Love." It was to have been their big hit together.

Big brother Foxley "I'm-so-famous" Dovercourt rushes in after her. "Pandora!" he puffs. "You can't come in here!"

"Oh, can't I? Just watch me. Yoo-hoo! Stanley!!"

A middle-aged man at the urinals snaps his head round in astonishment before zipping up and rushing out.

"Come out, Stan, you little salami gobbler! I know you're in here!" She bangs open the cubicle doors. "I've travelled thousands of miles to apologize to your little bisexual ass. The least you can do is . . . oh, I'm sorry!"

Perched on one of the toilets is a skinny young man in a black turtleneck and green Reeboks.

"I was just looking for . . ." she explains. ". . . um . . . Where did you get those shoes?"

"Well . . . I . . ."

Pandora knows full well where he got them. Off the feet of her ex-boyfriend, Stanley Park, that's where. There's no mistaking the friendship beads threaded on the laces. They spell out her name: PANDORA, in purple, green, and yellow.

A dark thought crosses her mind. "What have you done with him?!"

The guy smiles. Nervously. "He . . . he's fine," he gulps. "I think."

"I think not," retorts Pandora. "Stay right where you are. I'm calling the cops. Grant!"

She spins around. Her brother's at the doorway, along with a growing crowd.

"I wouldn't worry about calling security, Pandy," he calls, a tinge of triumph entering his voice as he gestures at the uniforms behind him. "They're already here."

The Stroke of Midnight

"This isn't funny!"Pandora screams at her brother as she is carted off by the police. "Why are they arresting me? They should be arresting him!"

She points an accusing finger at the slim young man with a pudding-basin haircut who is emerging from the bus station washrooms. "That dweeb killed Stanley! He stole his shoes! He . . ."

Pandora is thrust, regardless, into the dark hole of the paddy wagon and the stench of thousand-year-old vomit. The doors slam shut. Her ears ring.

Bloody hell! What a way to spend New Year's, she thinks. A few moments go by. She sniffs. Well, look on the bright side: at least they hadn't confiscated her guitar.

In the darkness, she picks out a tune.

"Ever since my boyfriend left me . . ."

A bubble of sorrow forms in her throat. She tries again.

"It doesn't matter where you go or what you do . . ."

But it does matter. Ever since Stan started showing a preference for boys instead of her, it's mattered. It's mattered so much that she crossed the country to get him back. OK, so perhaps she shouldn't have stuck a dead fish in his luggage.

The paddy wagon lurches off. Pandora is jolted from her seat and bangs her head against the wall.

"Oh, the pain of lo-oving you . . ."

▼

In Stanley Park's short career as a homosexual, he's managed to have sex in some unusual places, but none quite so strange as the interview room at the police station.

Left to their own devices, the squeegee kid and he had gone at it with a peculiar combination of trepidation and gusto. What could the police do? Arrest them?

As it turns out, it's over half an hour before they're interrupted, and by that time they are well sated. Twice, in fact.

"All right, you two. Put your clothes back on," barks an officer. "It's time to book into your hotel room for the night."

Their luxury suite for the evening proves to be a ten-by-ten cell, shared with seven others. Across the aisle, the chimpanzee has a cubicle all to itself. It seems quite happy, lolling about on its little bench, working away at an orange. Every so often it looks up and smiles like some beatific monk.

"What's he got to be so happy about?" wonders Stan.

"It's a *she*," growls a guy from the corner. "*Pan troglodytes*, female."

All further postulation as to why and how this simian lady has ended up in a holding cell on New Year's Eve is thwarted by someone screeching blue murder at the end of the corridor.

Stan recognizes the voice.

In a few seconds, his suspicions are confirmed, when a ragtag flurry of purple-and-green hair is marched into view between two stern and unyielding officers.

"Pandora!"

▼

Interlude

On the tropical South Sea Island of Mummichog, the mysterious woman helps herself to another cocktail. What cares she for the time? Hers is a life of leisure and relaxation. Civilization may be buzzing away furiously on the other side of the globe, but here, where she is known only as "Whatserface" by the locals, she marks time by the number of margaritas consumed.

The phone at her elbow rings. An intrusion. She glares at it. After four rings she changes its tone to a gentle chirping which she can pretend is the mating call of a tropical bird and is thus easily ignored.

The pool boy pokes his head around the corner.

"Lunchtime!" he sings.

Whatserface sighs.

What a life.

End of interlude

▼

"Stan!"

Pandora can't believe her eyes. After all this running around, all this searching in washrooms, being arrested, and suffering the indignities of having the strings of her guitar removed (supposedly for her own safety, in case she tries to garrote herself with them) – here he is!

"Stan, I'm so sorry about the fish!"

She is tossed into the cell opposite. As unstrung as her guitar, she clings to the bars, playing out a jail-cell drama.

"Stan. I love you."

Her confession has a strange effect. He's laughing at her! In fact, the whole gangbanging whack of drunks and dregs are laughing at her!

"Well, really, I don't see what's quite so funny!"

She turns to hide her fury and comes face to mug with a chimpanzee. It's blowing kisses at her. A chimpanzee. Wearing diapers and a Happy New Year tiara.

"Happy Wacky New Year, Monkey!" shouts Stanley, exploding into a guffaw as Pandora's eyes blink six billion times.

"Hey . . . is it midnight, yet?" someone asks.

"My watch says two minutes to."

"Mine says two minutes past."

"Mine says you've got another eight hours," mutters Pandora, "but then I screwed up when I got on the plane."

Someone decides that it's close enough to midnight as to make no odds and yells out, "Happy New Year!"

The cry is taken for truth. Cheers and hollers echo down the hallway from voices unseen. In the boys' pen across the way there are hugs and kisses. Pandora can't help but notice Stan spending a long time smooching at the lips of another young man. A tear rolls down her cheek.

She feels a tug on her smock. It's the chimp.

"What do you want, you ugly . . ."

But the chimp isn't going to let her get away with it that

easily. A hairy arm whips behind Pandora's neck and she is yanked towards pursed lips.

Her New Year's wish has come true. Pandora Begbie is not only reunited with her ex-boyfriend, but also gets a big wet one. Right up her nose.

Foxley Dovercourt rides through the freezing streets on his moped. He feels a tad guilty that he isn't going to the police station to rescue Pandora. Screw it. It's New Year's Eve. He's going to the bathhouse.

A RIDE program stops him outside the Holiday Inn.

"Is this your helmet, sir?"

"Well . . . er . . ." Foxley has to admit that it isn't; that he's only wearing the damned thing because his glasses are stuck inside. It's a long story, inexpertly told, despite Foxley's three years' training in the dramatic arts.

"Hand it over," demands the cop.

In one easy move the glasses come out.

"There you go."

"Thanks."

The cop writes him out a ticket for riding without a helmet and waves him on.

Eighty dollars in the hole, Foxley phut-phuts away, wondering whether this is an auspicious way to begin the New Year or not.

At least it's not snowing.

spring
beaver fever

(A Bureaucratic Fantasy Manual)

S pring! Forget nasty old winter – the snowstorm, the burst water pipes, the two weeks of flu – obliterate all those memories immediately. The yearly roller coaster of Life gears up for another bash at the wheel. Make way for the new!

Ha! Nothing really changes.

Judy Church is still on the treadmill, logging in the nine-to-five, riding the peasant-packer transit, fixing her brown-bag lunches, attending her Friday twelve-step meetings. The occasional night out with the girls. It's all the same old, same old, she thinks. Half a century of surprises and it's all come down to this: Birthday Duty.

Judy works (or, more accurately, is tolerated) in the Personnel Department at the law conglomerate Brunswick, Tecumseh & Yonge. Spread out over six floors in one of the beehive skyscrapers downtown, BT&Y boasts over four hundred employees, which means that on any given day, someone is likely celebrating a birthday. One of Judy's chores is to organize the festivities. Balloons, cake, whip-round, depending. The schedule is generated by computer, which, ever since the company tested its Y2K compliance, is a frigging nightmare. Some employees are, apparently, over a hundred years old.

Judy stares at her monitor in dismay. "Does a temp get a cookie or a pastry?"

Her boss, Mr. Baldwin, glances up from his newspaper. "The cookie," he snarls. "If they've been here longer than three months, they get a balloon on a stick. And a card if their work merits it." He turns back to his crossword, resenting the interruption.

Judy pats her lacquered coif for reassurance. If her eyebrows weren't permanently depilated into a look of painted shock she'd betray her disapproval of a system that measures people by productivity. Or is it merely Mr. Baldwin that she despises so much?

"No card, then," she decides. "It's Whatserface in accounting."

"Whatserface?" Mr. Baldwin's velveteen ears perk up like a cocker spaniel's. "Is she still here? I told you to terminate her last week. Really, Judy, you must try to keep more on the ball!"

▼

Interlude

Thousands of miles away, far from the hustle and bustle of Western Civilization, the sun beats down on the South Sea Island of Mummichog – a restful, tranquil, unspoiled refuge. Some would call it a true paradise on earth.

The mysterious woman known as "Whatserface "sits, as per usual, at the poolside bar. Her collagen-implanted lips pucker at the rim of her margarita, scrunching gently against the salt crystals.

She sighs and casts her tired, restretched eyes to the horizon, where a bird flits in the sunshine. She ponders the wonders of life insurance for a moment before trying to snag a renegade ice cube in the bottom of her glass.

The phone at her elbow purrs like a tropical bird. She considers ignoring it, then reaches out with a lazy, taloned hand.

"Hello?" She pops the ice cube into her mouth as a tinny voice squawks away in her ear. "Yup. Sure, I'll still be here in half an hour."

Hmph. Where else was she to go?

She slams down the phone. She chews the ice cube noisily. A scowl spreads like a twisting drain across her face.

"Damn!"

She sits there for a couple of seconds, desperately trying to keep a grip on herself. But it's no good; the reality of her situation is too strong. Bang goes her relaxing day by the pool. Judy fucking Church wants to pay a visit.

Angrily she wipes out her glass with a paper napkin before stashing it back into her desk drawer. She then flips her computer monitor from the tropical island screen saver to the January spreadsheet, yanks out a hefty file folder, slips her feet into her pumps, stuffs a pencil in her mouth and pretends to focus on her work.

With a bit of luck she'll be able to give the impression that she's been hard at it all morning.

End of Interlude

▼

Once a year, every year, as the earth hinges around the March equinox, Amelia Sackville divests herself of her winter identity. She goes through her wardrobe, chucking out everything without a designer label. Last year's lime greens, the chunky platform shoes, the whole pixie drum 'n bass look. Who did she think she was kidding at her age!

Her address book gets the same treatment. Anyone who reminds her of the past six months gets erased. Life is too short. And the raver-chick girlfriend, currently puking her guts up in the bathroom? It goes without saying – she'll be the first to go.

The table at the exclusive restaurant is already booked. Amelia intends to drop the bomb over a genteel luncheon – the civilized way. For someone in her mid-forties, pretending to be someone in her mid-twenties, Amelia is so Old School about these things.

It helps to be independently wealthy.

"Are you quite done in there?" she yells from her bed. "It sounds like you're sluicing the drains from here to Etobicoke!"

Silence. Then more stomach-wrenching orchestrations.

"Hey Willy!" she screeches. "Do you have to be so fucking repulsive first thing!"

She sneers at the bedside table, at the cluster of fingernail parings on the cigarette pack. How gauche. Sometimes she wonders how she picks 'em. Perhaps if she soaked the clippings in toilet paper and put them on a saucer on her windowsill, she'll be able to germinate herself a new girlfriend. Homegrown Willow. Hydroponic Chickweed.

The toilet flushes, announcing Willow's return. She appears – clinging to the doorway like Calvin Klein kiddie-porn flotsam –

dark heroin smudges beneath her eyes, her knees shaking like those of a newborn foal.

"I'm sorry, Amelia," she pants. "Did you, like, say something?"

She staggers across the debris of last night's carpet party and festoons onto the bed. Amelia inches herself away as if she'll get contaminated.

This drugged-out rave-scene groove she's been playing all winter has become tedious. Repulsive even. She deserves better.

"Here." She launches herself off the bed and tosses a housecoat at Willow. "Make yourself decent. You've got a lunch appointment in an hour."

With a flick of her Bic, Judy Church lights the third cigarette of her coffee break, not daring to look at her wrist-watch. She's taken fifteen minutes already, and could easily take another quarter of an hour. She's on a menthol nicotine binge.

More importantly, she's avoiding Whatserface in Accounting and the all-important pink-slip talk. Oh, how she hates having to fire anyone! Even a temp.

Blue smoke drifts towards the ochre-stained ceiling.

The Smoking Lounge is so claustrophobic. It's dominated by a stack of wheezing SmokeGuzzler™ air filtration systems. At less than thirty square feet, you can tell the room was originally intended to be a stock cupboard.

Of course, it's breaking every city bylaw to have a smoking area in the workplace, but Mr. Baldwin of Personnel prefers his still-addicted staff to pop into a secret fumarole rather than vanish outside the building – much too close to the temptations of shopping malls and bicycle couriers for his liking.

On the whole, thinks Judy, it's not a bad company to work for, is BT&Y. They do their best to keep a human face. She could do without that Mr. Baldwin, though.

On the stroke of twenty past, Monica, Stephanie, and Lenore (from word processing, purchasing, and the mail-room respectively) burst in. They tote a thick bridal catalogue (Monica's getting married in August) which they dump on the groaning coffee table as they light up.

"You're here late, Jude," pipes Monica, flipping through the kitchenware section. "What's up?"

Ever since she switched to menthols to ease herself back into the habit of smoking after a five-year quit, Judy Church has realized that the Smoking Lounge is the fulcrum of office gossip.

"I'm plucking up my courage," she confesses. "I have to fire Whatserface."

The wedding party pauses in its routine and exchanges knowing glances. "Whatserface in accounting? You mean the temp? Isabella? You're firing her?"

"The one. The same. She's history." Judy nods seriously as she grinds out her cool-as-a-mountain-stream cigarette. "And it's her birthday tomorrow."

"Oh, that's so awful!" chants the trio in mock-pained chorus. Judy wallows in the hypocrisy. Then, having announced her news to the company Hydra, she hauls herself out of her chair.

All she has to do now is carry out the deed.

Otello's is, appropriately, one of those suffocating restaurants with valet parking, linen napkins and honey-basted duck ovaries. For lunch, it caters to the blue-blazer and old-school-tie crowd. There are attendants in the washrooms.

Amelia Sackville has her annual table by the fountain. It is from this vantage point, with the stunning atrium view, that she goes through the yearly ritual of dumping her girlfriend of the season. This time around it's Willow Withrow, a rather scuzzy rave kid, who is three hours into a scalding hangover, complicated by menstrual cramps.

"It's, like, a bit stuffy, eh?" comments Willow, studying the menu.

Amelia gags inwardly at the word "like." The girl uses the word ubiquitously – it must be nice to live your life inside a simile.

"Have whatever you want," she beams. "My treat."

Willow gives her a nasty, street-urchin kind of look. Amelia shudders. Now that she's getting rid of her, she wonders what the attraction was in the first place. It had to have been the sex.

"You must try the marzipan oyster dip. It's delicious," she croons.

"Don't they have, like, some dry toast?" Willow quells a pale burp. "I'm feeling a bit off today, if it's all the same to you."

Lunch arrives with an ostentatious display of separate waiters for the vegetables, wine, and croutons. Amelia negotiates her way through a bowl of bouillon, a Waldorf salad, and a plate of calf brains *fines herbes*, while Willow nibbles the edges off some Melba toasts.

Amelia launches into her well-oiled speech about "going their separate ways" and "giving each other space." She bolsters her argument with references to Spiritual Needs and Life Goals. It's only when she reaches the details of what to do with the keys to the penthouse, that she looks into Willow's sunken eyes and gets the uneasy feeling that none of what she's saying is having any impact.

"Have you honestly heard a word I've been saying?"

Willow shakes her head, as if loosening a marble. "I'm sorry," she apologizes. "Did you, like, say something?"

"Damn right," says Amelia, in exasperation. "It's over, sweet-heart. Time to pack your things."

Silence.

"It's Spring," she continues. "I'm sick you. I never keep my girls beyond a season. This is the kiss-off. B*on appétit.*"

Aha. It's sunk in. Was that the sound of an elastic band snapping, or Willow's brain?

The freshly dumped Willow wipes her mouth with an Egyptian linen napkin. She folds it and places it carefully on her plate.

"Wow," she says, eventually. "You really are, like, a nasty old cunt, aren't you?"

"Isabella?" Judy Church pokes her friendly head around the door. "Can I have a word?"

"Uh-huh. Just a moment."

With a belaboured flourish, Isabella types a staccato of

keystrokes into her computer before swiveling round to face the music.

"Um." Judy hovers somewhere between the filing cabinet and the printer, unable to anchor herself. "Um . . . we really needed the January disbursements finished last month, Isabella. Now I know Mr. Baldwin's talked to you about this before. I'm afraid we're going to have to . . ."

"It's not my fault; it's the computer." Isabella snaps and turns back to her screen. She wiggles her mouse around. "It's gnarled everything from last week, you know. I can't get into the files."

"Gnarled?"

"Yup. Gnarled."

As if by way of punctuation, a little bomb dialog box appears – then the entire screen plummets into a zillion hieroglyphs of static.

Judy tries again. "You can take two weeks' pay in lieu of notice."

Isabella gapes at her monitor.

Judy sucks her teeth, staring at the floor, trying not to look Isabella in the eye. Now that she's here, now that she can see how impossible the computer system is to work with, now that she's said what she came to say, she can feel the emotion well up. She and Isabella are around the same age. They've been through much the same wars, she can tell. Life is so cruel.

"Thank you, Judy," purrs Isabella after a protracted silence.

"Um . . ." A tear rolls down Judy's cheek. "You know I haven't ordered your birthday cookie for tomorrow yet, but if you feel like swinging by . . ."

"Oh?"

"Would you like the chocolate chip or the macadamia nut?"

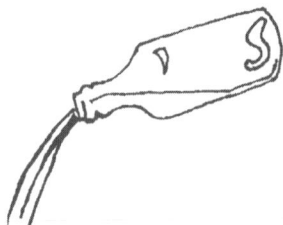

Birthdays are like subway trains. Some of them are soft rubber-wheeled dreams that glide through the stations of Life, punctually and efficiently picking up passengers. Others are nightmares of being stuck in some tunnel, in the dark, late for work, and you just know there's an electrical fire or a psychopath with a bomb in the next carriage.

Isabella Sherbourne's fifty-something'th birthday is of the latter type. Her birthday train got derailed at the depot. Yesterday she lost her job at the hoity-toity law firm of Brunswick, Tecumseh & Yonge. Forced to work as a beancounter all winter long because her husband had gone and died without so much a penny in life insurance, the only way she'd managed to get through those cold, harsh months was to pretend that she was on some South Sea island, a fantasy she denies cost her the job. It was that Mr. Baldwin from Personnel who had it in for her.

Last night she drank her way through a commiserating lagoon of tequila. This morning she looks and feels like the worm in the bottom of the bottle. She made the comparison check in the bathroom mirror. If they think she's going to put in an appearance today to sort out their disbursements, they have another think coming.

Isabella groans, loosens the elastic straps of her

BeautyDoze™ sleeping mask, and staggers to her little kitchenette to turn on the coffee machine. Upstairs, she can hear young Brock careening around the house. Living in the basement of the Bloor household is like living in Bedlam, but at least it's cheap. And compact. She has everything she needs close at hand, including her own private entrance so she can take Carlo II for walkies in the park without disturbing the rest of the house.

"Sorry, Carlo," she rasps, eyeing the dog leash hanging from its hook on the wall. "You'll have to hold onto your business until after coffee. Mommy's got a hangover."

Carlo II produces a high-pitched Chihuahua growl. He then aggravates his full bladder by chasing his tail round and around the kitchen-table leg before relieving himself.

Isabella stares at the spreading puddle of doggie urine across the kitchen tiles. The phone rings upstairs.

"It's for you, Bella!" shouts Marg Bloor, rapping on the basement door. "It's work! Something about a chocolate chip cookie?"

A malicious bubbling noise catches Isabella's attention. Coffee grounds ooze all over her counter. It is going to be one of those days. Happy Fucking Birthday.

Amelia Sackville snores like a Disney dragon. She sprawls on her Empress bed in her penthouse apartment, saliva horking up and down her oesophagus. She's having a well-deserved rest having dumped her girlfriend the day before. Oh, there had been tears! Oh, there had been such a scene in the restaurant!

The only way to calm Willow down had been to take her home, get her drunk, and give her a farewell fuck. It was breaking every rule in Amelia's book to do this, of course, but seeing as their relationship had been of the party kind to begin with, it only seemed fitting to end it on a similar note.

Now she's sleeping it off. A smile plays across her lips as her dreams play metaphors of new beginnings and fresh seasons.

If she were awake, however, this sense of well-being would soon vanish.

If she were awake, she'd snap a bra strap.

If she were awake, she'd fracture her manicure.

But, thanks to 25mg of Rohipnol surreptitiously dumped in her last cocktail, Amelia ain't gonna be openin' her eyes any time soon.

Tiptoeing around her, scarcely able to contain her glee, a shadowy figure brandishes a pair of scissors. *Snip!* The sleeves of a Chanel jacket fall to the floor. *Snap!* Chewing gum gets worked into a blue-fox fur. *Shh!* Whipped cream and oven cleaner ambush the underwear drawer.

Willow Withrow is exacting her revenge.

The computers are down. Again. May as well take another smoke break, thinks Judy Church. The Personnel Department at Brunswick, Tecumseh & Yonge can get along quite well without her for ten minutes.

Besides, Mr. Baldwin is having a nervous breakdown, and Judy doesn't want to be around when he cracks. He takes life way too seriously. Imagine! He called up Whatserface, fired her again, and told her she had to pay for her birthday cookie! What kind of anal-retentive psychosis is that?

It's enough to make you want to sing a hymn.

"I'm taking my break five minutes early," announces Judy, grabbing her purse. "If you want me, I'll be down in the lounge."

"Have you arranged for a new temp yet, Judy?" demands Mr. Baldwin. "There's a three-month backlog of disbursements that has to be cleared by Easter, you know."

Judy knows.

On the twenty-second floor she goes through an unassuming door to the rear of the staff kitchen, along a corridor and past the photocopier. The smoking lounge. If you can find it, you deserve your cigarette.

The wedding triumvirate (Monica, Stephanie, and Lenore) is already in there puffing up a lung. With a fourth. A sweet wisp of a raver girl with crazy hair and huge doe eyes.

With a start, Judy recognizes this newcomer from the dyke bars. One of those magnetic faces that kick-starts the old labia.

"Oh hi, Judy, you're down early, eh?" blurts Lenore. "This is my sister, well, my half-sister, actually, Willow. Willow, this is Judy . . . from *Personnel* . . ."

Judy waves away the introduction with her hand. She sits down and sparks a menthol. Be still her beating diaphragm! Lesbians in the office! She thought she was the only one.

"Like, don't I know you from somewhere?" asks half-sister Willow, squinching her nose.

Thanks to her painted eyebrows, Judy's face never betrays emotion.

"I think we may have shared a cab ride once," she dares.

"Right!" lies Willow. "I remember. Small world. Like, wow."

"Isn't that funny!" interrupts Stephanie, suddenly inspired.

"We were just talking about you, Judy. Is that job still open in accounting?" She grimaces, showing off the braces on her teeth. "Willow's got experience."

Willow shrugs and smiles.

"Really?" asks Judy, blood rushing to her head. "Is that a fact?"

The high-speed elevators that whisk people to the
offices of BT&Y can be a frightening experience. Especially if, like Isabella Sherbourne, you're loaded. Drunk as a skunk and it's only just gone noon. But Isabella doesn't care. It's her birthday. She may have gotten the pink slip from her pink-collar job yesterday, but, since she grifted all winter for these corporate ingrates, she's going to claim her chocolate chip fucking birthday cookie if it's the last thing she does.

"Floor twenty-two," announces the elevator in its mechanical voice.

Isabella's neck-tucks recover from the G-forces as she disembarks from the car. Her ankles buckle on the plush carpet in the reception area.

The door still opens to her magnetic security card – good – they haven't expunged her from the system yet. Slurring a drunken happy birthday song to herself, she negotiates the corridors that lead to her accounting department cell. Once or twice she loses her way and has to take a swig of tequila to get her bearings.

Soon, like rediscovering a bad fantasy, she is there: in the stinky hole they'd dumped her in for three months to sort out the January and February disbursements. Or to sip cocktails in the luxury bar of an elegant hotel on the South Sea island of Mummichog. Depending on your point of view.

Whichever way you look at it, there are still no balloons, no festive birthday decorations around her work station. No choco-late chip cookie. Just a skinny slip of a girl perched on what once was her poolside bar stool.

"Who are you?" she demands, her drunken eyes wobbling almost down to her cheekbone implants. "And where's my fucking birthday cookie?!"

The midday sun blasts, unforgiving, into Amelia Sackville's pent-house bedroom. She wakes in an instant, a fragrant smile on her lips. Yesterday she'd given her loser girlfriend the brush-off. Last night was the best night's sleep she's had in months. She breathes a lungful of sweet air and comforts herself with a moan.

The mood coagulates on her face with a cough. She bounds out of bed.

"The little bitch!"

The place stinks. A combination of Chanel, D&G, Lagerfeld – could that be oven cleaner? How could she have slept through this? Everywhere: a toxic fog.

Amelia flings open the bathroom door to come pheromone to eyeball with the proof of disaster. Two smashed perfume bottles and a jug of bleach are in the sink, their aromas mingling obscenely. The mirrors are daubed with lipsticks and foundations, the towels are soaked and smeared with liquid mascaras and face creams. Festive ribbons of toilet paper high and low. If there was a soundtrack to this scene, it would be a strident Hitchcockian Samba violin.

It's worse in the kitchen. Mountains of upended foodstuffs. Add some bongo drums playing a rising beat. Flour. Ketchup.

Minor seventh chord on brass. There's a message.

Dear mature lesbian . . . Amelia scans her eye down the scrawled note, skipping over the perfect syntax and the harsh barbs. When she gets to *enjoy your snooze – love Willow*, she knows how come she slept through the whole carnage.

The nightcap glass still beside the bed has a faint aroma to it. Amelia raises an eyebrow in recognition. The smell matches the plastic taste in the back of her throat.

"Christ!"

Amelia Sackville slumps on her bed and bursts into tears. Not from remorse. Nor from any medical cause. No. She weeps because Willow makes a heart over the *i* when she signs her name.

Youth can be so cruel.

Judy is in the smoking lounge when Mr. Baldwin bursts in. For him to enter this domain of the addicted has never before been known.

"Judy!" he whispers, his ears tinged with crimson. "I thought you fired Whatserface!"

"I did," retorts Judy.

"Well, she's creating a scene in accounting right now!"

Mr. Baldwin stands there like a prize sausage, shaking, and

gesturing meekly at the doorway. Clearly he expects Judy to scamper to the rescue.

Judy, however, takes her time. She finishes her cigarette. Then she walks. Casually. Down the corridor. A right. A left. Another left. Out of sobriety and into the heart of a drunken flashback.

"Cooo-kie, cooo-ooookie!"

Isabella Sherbourne, the defective temp, is dancing the fandango on the January and February disbursement files. The woman is soused to the gills, screaming to the heavens.

"Where's my birthday coo-oo-kie!! I want my shit-stinking chocky-chip birthday coo-oooo-kie!"

For Judy Church, this is a replay of why she divorced her alcoholic husband. Almost word for word, scene for scene.

Mr. Baldwin, pushing through from the rear, all elbows and shirt cuffs, opts for the confrontational approach.

"Miss Sherbourne," he demands, his pink neck bulging over his collar. "Have you been drinking?"

"What of it?"

The bottle of tequila is brandished aloft. Unfortunately, much like an exercise club, once the swing has started, the momentum can't be stopped. Luckily, Mr. Baldwin is vaguely familiar with a couple of self-defence moves. In one messy moment they are both on the carpet.

"Your birthday was . . . removed . . . from the . . . computer!" huffs Mr. Baldwin from behind an elbow lock.

"Get this damned pool boy off me," screeches Isabella, before launching into "La Cucaracha."

Observing all this, Judy is miles away, caught in her own memories. If she's not careful, she'll break out in a hymn. She looks around her for something to hold on to, some epiphany or other.

Miracle upon miracles! She is saved – not by Jesus, but by the new temp, cute little Willow Whatsername, who is backed into a corner, a damsel-in-distress look on her face.

Their eyes meet across the kerfuffle. Judy's head swims.

"Stick this in your frigging computer!" warbles Isabella, clambering over the stolid bulk of Mr. Baldwin. She chugalugs some more tequila before upending the remainder – a good third of it – all over the laser printer.

"Bottoms up!"

A puff of blue smoke, an electric crackle, and the machine dies. Mr. Baldwin wails.

But throughout the mayhem, Judy's eyes remain locked with Willow's. Magic. The unmistakable promise of sex. The surge of desire. Kismet à Lesbos. The scrapping temp and head of Personnel may as well be a million miles away.

Could this be love?

Amelia Sackville strides around her brand-new water-front condo overseeing the arrival of her furniture. Satisfied with the placement of the couch, she pours herself a slopping glass of red wine, seats herself and stares out, gently bleezed, over the lake.

What a view!

She has a lot to be thankful for. Strange: every year she feels the same. Spring. A renewal of life, a new start. Thank God she got out of that awful sixties penthouse apartment.

"Over there," she tells the moving boys, pointing clearly to the desired spot. "Careful with that! That's an antique!"

In the back of her mind she knows there's something left undone, that each spring after she's gone through this emotional turmoil, moves into a new place, starts all over again – there's this sneaky feeling that – how do those New Agers put it? – that unless she learns from her mistakes, she is doomed to repeat them.

But Amelia would sooner split a nail than for such a warning to have any impact. For her, mistakes are a sickness. And as soon as she's better, she forgets she was ever ill.

One of the movers drops a crate of books, the sweat bursting from his brow. Amelia wonders whether she ought to offer him a glass of water.

"You idiot! You're lucky there's nothing breakable in there!"

It must contain her heart.

She sighs. Winter's abominable girlfriend is but a memory now. Fading tracks in the snow. God, what a creature! With a nasty vindictive streak!

The gum will never come out of the blue fox. She'll have to have it patched.

Well, no more. Next time, she'll be more cautious when she dumps her flings. Just toss 'em out. No more fancy lunches. And never, never to make the stupid mistake of a mercy fuck again. Phew! That one had cost her. What with the cleanup of the old apartment, the runaround to replace her wardrobe, the real-estate agents – well! It had set her back almost twenty thousand.

She has to admit, however, that it's kept her occupied. It's been kind of fun.

"Mind the paintwork!"

With the damage and the mess that little monkey made at the old place, she could have pressed charges. She could have exacted her own revenge. She could have done whatever she wanted. She could have made a discreet phone call and had the little bint's ovaries snipped out, just like the arms of that Chanel jacket.

But she hasn't and she won't.

Life will be just dandy if she never claps eyes on that Willow Withrow again. The girl will land on her feet, surely. That type always does. She'll probably make some bull-dyke very happy.

Amelia screws up her nose at the wine. It tastes a bit acetic. A touch bitter. But at forty-five dollars a bottle, she'll force herself to drink it. And enjoy it.

"Will you assholes be careful with that china! Jesus! Wherever do they find you people?!"

Interlude

The South Sea island of Mummichog has an exclusive nursing home on the west side of the mountain overlooking the bay. Here the residents can sit on the verandah, take in the sun, and convalesce.

The mysterious woman known as "Whatserface" by the locals, has her own favourite corner, by the overgrown gazebo, where the toucans hop on the wrought-iron balustrade and from where once a day, just before sunset, she can watch as the children from the island school perform their calisthenics in the field below.

A nursing sister, crisp in her white habit, approaches the mysterious woman and gently touches her shoulder.

"Did you take your medications today, Isabella?"

Isabella is startled from her reverie. She looks at the glass of water on the table beside her, at the little pill box, and furrows her extraordinary brow.

"I think so."

The nurse retreats. A flock of flamingos rises like a swirling pink cloud in the setting sun. Isabella sighs. Life is so wonderful. Now that they've fired that pool boy, perhaps tomorrow she'll go for a swim.

End of interlude

"So whatever happened to Whatserface?"

Judy Church looks up from her crossword, only slightly annoyed at the interruption. Her irritation melts at the sight of Willow Withrow's doe eyes. There are few things in life that get Judy's juices flowing. Having Willow at her elbow, girl Monday to girl Friday, is one of them.

"I'm sorry, Willy, what did you say?"

"Whatever became of that scary temp, Whatserface? Isabella Sherbourne, wasn't it?"

"Oh, her." Judy chews her pencil for a moment. "They put her in the nuthouse. Lithium for life."

She chuckles to herself. If it hadn't have been for Isabella's drunken tirade, poor old Mr. Baldwin would never have quit, Judy would never have taken his place, and Willow wouldn't be where she is now: in Judy's old job in the Personnel Department at Brunswick, Tecumseh & Yonge.

"Well, the computer wants, like, a forwarding address for her T4 slip. Where do I send it?"

"Screw the computer," jokes Judy. "It's never been the same since we ran the Y2K test on it."

"Like, who needs computers anyway?"

"Precisely."

Aha. Judy finishes off the crossword with a satisfying nine-letter word. She has a few minutes to spare. Perhaps she could check down the Birthday List to see who is going to be celebrating tomorrow. Perhaps she could put the moves on Willow. Again.

"Do you fancy a bite somewhere nice after work today, Willy? My treat."

"Hmm. Let's go Dutch. Treats make me nervous."

Judy feels a surge of sexual prowess. Drivin' the donkey with Willow is proving to be a welcome addition to her life.

With a bit of luck it could last all summer.

"Did I ever tell you about the time me and my twelve girlfriends won the Best Costume Award at the Halloween Ball?"

"No!" Willow's face is full of admiration. Flushed. "Like, did you really?"

kamikaze sex party

(A Sci-Fi Steam Room Farce)

T he *Help Wanted* notice at The Gentleman's Quarters is permanent – painted onto the sign at the door. Right there, below *No Drugs, No Solicitation, No Women, No In-And-Out Privileges.* A right-wing Baptist might see it as a homosexual recruitment drive. The management, however, sees it as a necessary announcement. There's always a vacancy for someone willing to clean cubicles for minimum wage.

Over the past five months, Stanley Park (no longer fresh off the boat from the West Coast) has done the waitering thing, the bicycle courier thing, the Welfare thing, the busboy thing, the drug-dealing thing, and is now scraping the bottom of his gay barrel, so to speak, in an effort to pay his two-month-overdue rent thing. He's being trained in the fine art of towel folding. Origami it is not.

"And then you spray the room down with this." Gerrard Pape

holds up a bottle of industrial cleanser.

"Always wear rubber gloves," he advises. "And if there's Crisco on the mirrors, it'll form a poisonous gas that'll make you sterile in a week."

"No shit!"

They laugh, but it's not really funny.

In fact, the whole orientation session plays like a stand-up comedy routine, with the punchlines somehow removed. Never engage in eye-contact with a customer who's fried on crystal meth. Always carry the master keys. Look out for the guy with loose bowels in the steam room.

Stanley is coming to the conclusion that the real joke is either his six-dollar wage or his twelve-hour shift, no breaks. Beelzebub's minions surely get better working conditions. Stanley must have raped an Amish preacher in a past life to deserve this.

The sad truth: this is the only job available right now. Since he's not willing to remove his facial piercings or slap on a monkey suit (as if he had such a thing), then he has no option but to bite the bullet. He has to admit he's curious as to what goes on behind the curtain in the Land of Oz.

"Oh, and every four weeks you're gonna need one of those." Gerrard gestures at a wreath of garlic hanging on the wall behind the cash register. "Full moon, the place fills up with vampires and werewolves. Oh yeah – and there's a gun with silver bullets in the safe."

Stan can't tell if he's being kidded or not.

"Whaddya mean, they're not doing any more girls nights? That sucks!"

Liberty hoovers up a pyramid of ketamine from the back of a CD case. Her girlfriend, Rose, pours herself a sedate shot of vodka.

"No more girls nights at The Gentleman's Quarters," drawls Rose. "They're saying it was a one-time event. The creeps."

"Bisogydists!" complains Liberty, pressing a digit against her nostril. "Girls dight was the bost successful dight they've ever had – the place was packed to the glory holes – they're just jealous."

"Yeah," agrees Rose. "Jealous of the six-and-a-half-hour orgasm. That's probably it, y'know, Lib. Turnover. The guys get their rocks off and leave in three point six minutes. The girls stay there all night."

They sit and ponder their biological advantages. Ketamine drips down the back of Liberty's throat.

"So it's back to dark alleys and municipal saunas for us dykes, is it?" she moans, massaging her ankles. "Shit. And life was just starting to get interesting."

She's referring to a six-gal pileup behind the candy machine at The Gentleman's Quarters. The welts will take weeks to fade. Trophy bruises.

"You'd think," mutters Rose, "you'd think in a city with the highest per capita bathhouse ratio in the Northern Hemisphere, there'd be somewhere for us ladies to blow off some steam."

Liberty sets herself up another K-bump.

"I'll get us in," she vows. "Just you watch me."

▼

Lunchtime rush at Our Lady of the Perpetual Waters, and Alexander Church in Room 222 changes his pose. He adjusts his towel "just so" over his groin, tightens his stomach muscles, flexes his biceps above his head, and waits for True Love to pass his door. The chances are slim, but he'll take the nearest fucksimile.

He counts down mentally from twenty, after which, if anything promising has trolled by, he'll change his pose to something more provocative. One of The Hun's farmboys brought to life, for instance. If no one has taken his fancy in that twenty seconds, he'll close the door and sulk. After all, he isn't really supposed to be here. Murray would be insufferable if he found out.

Murray. Huh. It's an on-again off-again spin cycle with that fashionable kiwi fruit. Right now, it's supposed to be *on*, but judging by the number of Alex's visits to the steam baths over the past week, it'll soon be *off*. There are only so many excuses he can make before having to resort to honesty.

"I have to go for a walk."

"How come every time you go for a walk you come back stinking of chlorine and poppers?"

Murray's a good catch. But every so often Alex wants something different. Very different. Look what he's put up on the chalkboard in the washroom:

Naughty boy needs Daddy for old-fashioned discipline. Room 222.

Master Alexander Church is working through some parental issues. "3 . . . 2 . . . 1 . . . zero . . . 20 . . . 19 . . ."

He gives himself another twenty penalty seconds. Hopefully the father figure of his dreams will turn up in that time. He'd better. Holding this pose is giving him a charley horse.

If there is one being in this universe who can do six thousand things at once, it would have to be Cherry Beach. Right now she relaxes in the playroom and reads the classifieds from the newspaper whilst scoffing bonbons. She sits on a padded leather stool, with her six-inch heels resting on the Colonial Spanish Inquisition rack. Every so often she'll nonchalantly whip Handsome Jack's bare ass which hangs in the sling beside her.

"Kinky businessman, mid-fifties, (*whack*)," she reads, "seeks frisky playmates for extended torture sessions in well-equipped dungeon (*whack*). Hmm." She holds the paper out to where Handsome Jack can see it, lifts his blindfold and shows him the ad.

"They've gone and put it in the wrong section again," she says. "Long-term lesbians. Shall I call and complain or will you?"

"Hmmlbe chghmmwi."

"OK. Suit yourself."

She goes back to reading, whipping, and chocolate sampling. It doesn't take long before tedium sets in: a dull ache up along her wrist and straight into her brain.

It was too bad. Her nine months with Handsome Jack have run the gamut, the rack, and the Saint Andrew's Cross. Now they've settled into a rut. Even the magenta wand can't bring the spark back into their love life.

They crave something new. Something exciting. An audience?

"Hey look!"

Cherry flashes another page in Handsome Jack's beetroot face. *The Gentleman's Quarters: Full Moon Rubber Perv Night*.

"Whaddya think?"

"That sounds humiliating!" grunts Handsome Jack after Cherry removes his gag. "Let's give it a whirl."

"Room 222, it's time to check out or renew."

Stanley Park is working his first Full Moon shift at the Gentleman's Quarters. Things are starting to get a bit out of hand and his fellow cowpoke, Paisley, has vanished into some anonymous black hole on the second floor. There's a special promotion this evening: anyone wearing rubber gets in for half price. Condoms don't count.

It's about 11:30 in the evening, and a lineup is forming at the door. Stan tries to get into the rhythm of handing out the keys, towels, fuck kits, taking the money, but he isn't coordinated into the routine yet.

His blood pressure rises as he accidentally shortchanges someone.

"Look, I'm sorry," he blurts. "It's my first night on cash, OK?"

A tousle-headed blond guy arrives at the counter in the lounge area and starts pinging the bell.

Stan ignores him as he faces the next-in-line at his window. Now here's a quandary. He can't remember what the policy is about sex changes. No women, he remembers that. But transgenders? On a rubber fetish night?

"When's the party starting?" demands the guy in the lounge, almost banging the nipple off the bell.

"Quiet your horses!" yells Stan over his shoulder. "Can't you see it's a zoo in here tonight!"

"In that case, I'll take six more hours." A balled up twenty-dollar bill hits Stan on the back of the neck. "Room 222. Keep the change."

▼

"My, you're making a tragic time of it, aren't you?"

Cherry Beach smiles sweetly at the poor grunge kid behind the window and proffers a sharp fifty-dollar note.

"Look, I'm sorry. I don't think I'm allowed to let women, partial or otherwise, into this establishment. It's policy."

"Oh, I'm not female," says Cherry, lowering her voice and gently manipulating the truth. A little grey lie won't hurt anyone. She lets her PVC raincoat slip from her shoulders, revealing her open-breasted rubber corset.

"Then what are those . . . ?"

Quick as a flash, Cherry grabs one of the young man's hands through the open grillwork and forces it onto her breast. Squeeze. The soft vinyl compound pops in upon itself, as does the poor lad's brain, judging by the look in his eyes.

"If that doesn't classify as a rubber fetish," says Cherry, turning on the charm, "then I don't know what does."

"Uh. Ja. Right." He looks nervously over at Handsome Jack, as if wondering whether to continue the challenge, then thinks better of it. "What can I get for you?"

"We'll take the sling room if you'll be so kind."

"Um . . . both sling rooms are taken," says the harried lad. "But I think the double with the glory hole by the Jacuzzi is vacant. Yup. Do you want that one?"

"Ah, the bridal suite," says Cherry, turning to her companion. "What d'you think, Jackie-boy?"

Handsome Jack can only answer in grunts and wheezes. He's all trussed up from head to toe in black rubber, including a full gas mask, with a vinyl sports bag of goodies clutched in his manacled hands. He looks and sounds like a Satanic Teletubby.

"Ngh-mpph."

"We'll take it."

"Wheee!"

Liberty Hanna sits in the leather sling, kicks up her legs, and rocks with delight.

It had been surprisingly easy getting in. But then, as she catches her reflection in the ceiling mirror, she has to admit her slutty French-Canadian leather-boy drag is remarkably convincing. It's frightening what a moustache can do to perception of gender.

"C'est fantastique, Louis!" she gloats in an atrocious French accent. "Louis, yous are da genius!"

Louis is her alter ego for the evening. Louis was also the name of her pajama case when she was seven years old, but she's pretending she can't remember that.

She steadies herself in the sling while she sets herself up with a bump of K. *Toot-a-toot*. That done, she swings for a while on her back, enjoying the drug as it gives her an out-of-body, swinging-over-the-void experience. Residues of past reflections jump out at her from the mirror above (or is it below?), catching her in an orgasmatron warp. A waft of butyl nitrite hits her connoisseur's nostrils from somewhere down the corridor. Oh, she's going to enjoy this evening! She can't wait to see the looks on everyone's faces.

Oh, right. The others. Shit. She'd almost forgotten that she's on a mission.

Guiltily, Liberty breaks out of her drug oobe and dismounts from the sling. There's a whole crowd of grrls, wymmyn, dykes 'n' lesboes waiting outside at the back door to be snuck in. About fifty of them, last count.

The Gentleman's Quarters isn't gonna know what hit it.

"Hokay, Louis," she giggles, brandishing a pair of wire cutters. "Let's get dis show on da road!"

FF, WS, CBT, AA, NA, CLR . . . the chalkboard is full.

Cherry Beach casts her eye down the list of advertisers as she refills her water bottle. She makes mental notes, trying to impress the room numbers on her brain – trying to match up the visuals with the acronymic hype. She may even get lucky and hook a third or fourth for their party room.

Thus it is that her first pit stop is at Room 222, where the "naughty boy" looking for a "daddy" is snoozing face down on his cot, his ass beautifully on display. Just so. Cherry tiptoes into the room and gives the buns a playful whack with her riding crop.

She elicits a moan from the prostrate figure. So she repeats the gesture.

"Mmmm. MMMMMMMMM."

She cocks a discerning eyebrow. One of Cherry Beach's life skills, acquired over many years of necessary practice, is being able to distinguish one kind of moan from another. Her eyes narrow and flicker as she riffles through her mental Rolodex. Her eyelashes almost come unglued. She knows that moan.

She leans forward and purrs in an ear.

"Well, well, well. It's a small world, isn't it?"

The recumbent blonde gives a start, hastily covering his dwindling erection with a towel as he twists sharply round to face his intruder.

"Christ, it's Cherry Beach!"

"Shh! Not so loud," says Cherry, a finger to her lips. "I've got your Dad just down the hallway. I read somewhere you were looking for him."

Ever since the love of his life died last Pride Day, Donald Silverthorne has become more and more entrenched in the world of fetish sex. It began innocently enough with boots and cockrings, escalating through tit clamps and candle wax, finally ending up with his current obsession: autoasphyxiation. The noose.

A nervous man to begin with, this intimate dance along the edge of breath is, Donald knows, a dangerous pastime. He's tried to limit himself to chaperoned sessions, although that's been getting more and more difficult as his desires have escalated.

Potential partners (i.e. hangmen) tend to run screaming when he pulls out the thick black silk rope and the footstool.

But Donald has reached a point on his journey past caring. Everyone has to leave this vale of tears sometime, he reckons. He may as well be having fun when he goes.

Tonight is not only a full moon, but also rubber fetish party night at The Gentleman's Quarters. Donald has reserved his favourite room, the one with the ladder up the wall and the hooks in the ceiling. Perfect for his needs – so long as the beam holds.

His heart pounds as he sets up his rig. A year ago he would never have thought he'd be applying his Boy Scout know-how quite this way. But many and strange are the twists of the world.

You never know what kinks lie in wait for you around the next corner.

▼

There are two sets of washrooms. One with urinals and one without. Since women have only been allowed on the premises once before, it wouldn't be fair to call the latter "the ladies," although right now that's clearly what it is.

Fifty or so of the city's most daring lesbian ladies – those willing to put themselves on the line – are cramming themselves in there. They're sneaking in through the back door, which is kept open by our fifth columnist of the evening, Liberty Hanna in a shockingly convincing leather-boy drag.

"Shh! Not so loud!" she hisses through her moustache, as she ushers woman after woman in from the emergency exit, across the hallway, and into the washroom. "Don't let the pussy out of the bag quite yet!"

It's no smooth military operation, mainly because of the excitement of being somewhere they're not allowed. Truth be known, nobody really thought they'd get this far. They'd thought that Liberty would get discovered at the door, that she would snip the wrong wire on the emergency exit and the alarm would betray their presence. That someone would see them sneaking in. So many opportunities for failure and yet, it would appear, they've negotiated the minefield successfully.

"Woh," smiles Liberty, trying to get a handle on her palpitations. "Here we are! We're really here."

"Yeah," drawls Rose, stuffing her street clothes into a black garbage bag. "We're here. Stuck in the washrooms. Now what do we do?"

"Ah." Liberty sucks her bottom lip. "That's easy. Now we party!"

▼

Cherry Beach holds a finger to her mouth and gives Alex the ol' silent eye warning as she lets him into the double cubicle.

"Hey Jackie-boy!" she announces. "We have a visitor."

Handsome Jack is trussed and chained to the mattress. Hogtied, gas-masked, manacled, and bound in rubber, he looks ready to be served on a platter for Thanksgiving.

"I'm not sure about this," whispers Alex, nervously. "When I said that I wanted a Daddy, I didn't mean the real thing."

"All righty," says Cherry, ignoring him with matronly matter-of-factness. "Ground rules."

She launches into a spiel of the limits of play. Her mind is barely on the task, too full of the joke of the situation is she. What a coincidence! What happenstance! It's not often she gets to oversee a father-and-son team.

". . . And the safe word of the evening is . . ." She searches her brain for something suitable. Something pithy.

"The safe word – or rather, words – are 'Ernest Hemingway'."

Without further ado, she manipulates Handsome Jack into a crouched position, his haunches pointing heavenward. She then unsnaps his rubber bumflap, to reveal a pimpled derrière, and hands Alex the English Leather horsewhip.

"Go for it, dear" she whispers. "You know you've always wanted to."

"Now that you mention it," says Alex, tentatively, "there are a few unresolved issues between me and this freak."

At the sound of his son's voice, Handsome Jack's head jolts back in surprise. The eyes behind the gas mask oggle like an alien about to be autopsied. He wriggles. He struggles. But there's nothing he can do. He is, after all, in an uncompromising position.

Whack!

▼

Liberty Hanna pokes her head around the washroom door by the fire exit. Her false moustache and carefully applied crepe-hair stubble are starting to wilt with the heat and excitement. The coast is clear.

"OK, guys," she whispers over her shoulder. "Here we go."

The lesbian-packed washroom behind her is abuzz with beach towels, shower caps, flip-flops and swimsuits. Everyone is a-flutter with anticipation.

"Follow me."

And with that, she leads them, Pied-Piper-style, into the corridors of male exclusivity. No longer is there any hope of concealing their presence, and as they go, their chatter and laughter get louder. A few whoops of joy. A couple of shouts of glee.

Liberty yanks open a mirrored door, a gust of steam blasts in her face.

"Look out boys! We've arrived!"

▼

Ping! Ping! Ping!

The bell in the lounge is screaming for attention. A moustachioed University Queen is punishing it as if this would somehow remove the sour look from his face.

"Women in the steam room!"

"Oh, that's not a woman," says Stan. "They're rubber falsies. I checked."

"You didn't hear me properly, dear," the queen chides. "Wo-*men*. Plural. The place is rife with them."

By way of illustration, two topless bathing beauties appear, laughing, arm in arm as if wandering down the beach at St Tropez.

"Hi, fellas!" they warble. "Which way to the Jacuzzi?"

Her Majesty chokes back vindication while Stanley racks his brain trying to remember having opened the Gentleman's Quarters' hallowed doors to females. He's sure he didn't. Not even in a momentary relapse. Where had they sprung from?

"See!" snorts the Queen. "See! See! Toss them out!"

"*Jawohl, mein Führer,*" mutters Stan. "*Ich bin dein Hund!*"

▼

In the privacy of his room, Donald Silverthorne's vision blurs. The silken rope tightens around his neck. Every time his feet slip from their perch on the stool, a whistle sings through his ears and a shudder racks his body.

Another noise catches in his ear. It sounds like laughter. Cartoon laughter; giggling munchkins from another dimension, perhaps. It's difficult to tell in his wound-up state. He may well have stepped over the rainbow.

What a laugh if Mum could see me now, he thinks. She'd cash in her PFLAG card for sure if she saw him in this harness, these bands of leather holding his body in place, encircling his groin, this latticework of depravity. The noose.

He is alone.

His door is closed. Locked. Tonight Donald doesn't feel like explaining things to strangers – he's going straight for a rendez-vous with his animus. Another swing. The hook creaks in the ceiling. His vision melts as his weight pulls down on the rope. The munchkin laughter gets louder.

Ah, such tangible ecstasy!

"What's da problem? D'ere's no problem 'ere."

"Let me through, sir."

"You can't go in dere!"

Arms outspread, a leather boy bars Stan's way into the steam room.

"I work here."

"Den h'especially you can't go in dere."

The sound of female laughter fills the air. Three men, grimacing with horror and clutching their towels around their waists, skedaddle around the corner.

"Women!" yelps one.

"Mommy!" warbles another.

Oh please, thinks Stanley. He's had it with the craziness of the evening. He isn't being paid enough for this kind of hassle.

He eyes the Franco-leather boy. "Your moustache is slipping off your face, *mein Liebling*."

The leather lad's hand flies to his lip. He thinks for a moment, shrugs, then rips open his shirt, unravels a tensor bandage that's been holding breasts in place, and reveals himself to be a her.

"Surprise!" she beams, tits to the wind. "Buffalo gals go round the outside!"

At which point, the ceiling caves in.

Multiball!

No arcade game could ever match this fiasco. The collapsing roof sets off the sprinklers – it won't be long before the fire department turns up. Everywhere: men, women, towels, arms, legs, screeching and hollering, shocked bewilderment, up and down the hallways, scrabbling for clothes. The grrls have taken over the Jacuzzi and they're having a splash-fest. The place is alive. Chalk up another bull's eye for Santa Calamity.

Tilt!

Cherry Beach is in her element.

She stands in the eye of the storm, smiling like Pulcinella. The blood courses through her veins. Excitement! Yes! This is what she's been craving. Chaos.

Behind her, Handsome Jack makes a run for it. He staggers a few steps, falls, picks himself up again. Alex follows, whipping away in a frenzy.

"Oh, you like that don'tcha, huh?" W*hip, whip, whip.* "That's it. Don't stop now, when you're enjoying yerself, Pussy-Daddy!" W*hip.*

Handsome Jack is desperate to rid himself of his restricting costume. With a clawing motion he yanks at his rubber ties. Off comes the gas mask, revealing a face all red and sweaty, hair plastered to the cheek.

"Hemingway!" he pants, drawing oxygen noisily across his teeth. "Ernest Fucking Hemingway you little bastard!"

"Donald! Donald Silverthorne!"

Donald cracks his eyes open at the sound of his name. The voice is coming from the ceiling. Or is that the floor beneath his swinging feet? He can't tell. There's a cloud of dust and a load of rubble. The hooks in the ceiling must have given way. Damn.

Disappointed? Not really. For he knows in his heart of hearts that he's finally achieved something. He's dead.

By way of proof, a multicoloured leprechaun steps through a rippling vortex and into the room as if it were the most common occurrence in the universe. Clipboard in hand, he gives Donald the once over, then strokes his interdimensional whiskers.

"Karma tally," he chirps in a helium mezzo. "You have an accumulated total of 1,378 karma points, plus a bonus of 42 for killing a homophobe. What's your reincarnation preference?"

Donald swallows, strangely. "You mean . . . you mean I get a choice?"

"Well, you're limited to the animal or vegetable kingdom," comes the reply. "You'll need another 3,580 to be considered for the mineral categories. What's it to be?"

Faced with such enormous choice, Donald is speechless.

"Come on, come on!" snaps the diminutive afterlife official. "Ten seconds before we make the choice for you."

"Oh, I don't know!" blurts Donald. "I'm sure I'll make a cock-up of whatever I get, anyways."

"Yes, there is that," sighs the elf, ticking off a box on his list. "OK. Dust weevil it is."

"Dust weev . . . ?"

In the twinkling of an intergalactic eye, Donald Silverthorne is transmogrified.

The Gentleman's Quarters limps on. It's going to take more than the roof falling in, an autoasphyxiated suicide, a few dozen lesbian marauders and an uptight bunch of regulars for it to close its doors. Once the emergency crews have left and the hysteria has subsided, yellow caution tape is strung up, and it's business as usual.

"Fucking dust gets everywhere!" Gerrard Pape sprinkles Mr. Kwik Kleen into a pail and starts priming a mop.

Stan looks on sheepishly as he pulls on his jacket. "So. I'm off, then," he says.

"Sure I can't make you change your mind?" Gerrard attacks the floor with gusto. "Not even for another two dollars an hour?"

Stan zips up his jacket, grabs his skateboard. "You're joking, right?"

He doesn't wait for an answer.

Outside, the sun rises on a clear morning. There's a bite in the air. The streets are deserted; it's early yet. Stan breathes a deep, restoring moment, stilling himself, calming.

So he's quit his job. What now?

From his pocket he pulls out his shades. He cracks a fresh stick of gum. Flicks the wrapper down the storm grate. Heads east on his skateboard, grinning.

By the end of the block he's laughing aloud.

GREG KRAMER

Greg Kramer is an actor, artist, designer, director, playwright, as well as author of two novels: *the pursemonger of fugu* (shortlisted for the City of Toronto Book Award) and *Couchwarmer*.

After having sampled the delights of Vancouver and Toronto, Greg now lives in Montréal.